SMOKE SCREEN

SMOKE SCREEN

Lawrence Saunders

COACHWHIP PUBLICATIONS
GREENVILLE, OHIO

Smoke Screen, by Lawrence Saunders
© 2025 Coachwhip Publications edition
Introduction: © 2025 Curtis Evans
Cover image: © VBaleha

First published 1930
John Burton Davis, 1893-1970
Clare Ogden Davis, 1892-1970
CoachwhipBooks.com

ISBN 1-61646-600-6
ISBN-13 978-1-61646-600-8

INTRODUCTION
Curtis Evans

Lawrence Saunders was the author of three American detective novels in the early Thirties: *Smoke Screen* (1930), *The Columnist Murder* (1931) and *Devil's Den* (1933). In reality the pseudonymous name of Lawrence Saunders—recalling Gwen Bristow and Bruce Manning, authors, right around the same time, of *The Invisible Host* and three other mysteries—hid a married pair of journalists, John Burton Davis and Clare Ogden Davis. Constantly coming face to face with crime in their journalistic careers, reporters like Bristow and Manning and the Davises not unnaturally decided to try their hands at fictional murder.

John Burton Davis was born in Perryville, Missouri, in 1893 to newspaper editor John Brooks Davis and his wife Laurette Saunders Davis, whose maiden name Saunders provided half of the inspiration for "Lawrence Saunders." (The Lawrence half came from the maiden surname of Clare Ogden's mother.) Burt entered the school of journalism at the University of Missouri in 1913, but withdrew after only a year to convalesce from illness at balmy Brownsville, Texas. So did the young man inadvertently turn the key in the lock of the door to his life's great adventure.

In 1915 the *Brownsville Daily Herald* put Burt on its news staff and in 1916-17 the enterprising, bilingual cub

CLARE OGDEN DAVIS

reporter inveigled himself into serving as an interpreter with General Pershing's punitive Mexican expedition against the notorious revolutionary Pancho Villa. While the Great War, which soon ensnared the United States, continued to rage overseas in Europe, Burt worked at the *Houston Post* and lodged at the local YMCA. His draft registration card describes him as tall, of medium weight, with brown eyes and black hair.

1920 found Burt in Fort Worth employed with the *Record*, where he met spunky, redheaded "girl reporter" Clare Ogden, who worked in the Fort Worth office of the Dallas *Morning News* and was reputedly the first woman in Texas ever to cover police assignments for a newspaper. In classic film fashion Clare professed to loathe the tall, brash, black-haired newsman at first sight, later declaring of their initial meeting: "I saw him and asked somebody who is that scarecrow who thought he was a little tin god." Thirteen days later in full romcom fashion the little tin god proposed marriage to the pioneering newswoman and she accepted.

The Davis marriage, which never produced any children, was not without bumps in the road, however. "Surely we've had fights," Clare reflected in 1932, when the pair were promoting *Six Weeks*, a mainstream Reno divorce novel. "We've been near to divorce [ourselves] at least twice. . . . I think perhaps the thing that holds us together is the fact that neither has a better friend than the other."

The union of these two best friends, who after some years in New York (see below) returned to live in Austin, Texas, after World War Two, endured for a half-century. Clare suffered a debilitating stroke in 1965, forcing her to retire from the column in the Austin *American*, "In My Texas Garden," which she had written since 1951. Burt loyally kept it up himself for a year, pending Clare's promised return, but she never made it back. He died from

TWO GARDENERS—When Former Governor Miriam A. Ferguson, right, and her former press secretary, Clare Ogden Davis, new resi- dent of Austin, visited for the first time in many years, they talked of flowers and herbs and how to make a garden grow. (Staff Photo by Bill Monroe.)

1951

cancer at the age of seventy-six in April 1970 and Clare, still bedridden, finally passed away a month after her husband at the age of seventy-seven. It was a sad end to two distinguished and dynamic careers.

Clare Ogden had been born near Waco, Texas in 1892 to a pair of prosperous ranchers. She graduated in 1913 from Baylor College at Belton, a private Christian women's university (now the University of Mary Hardin-Baylor) and taught high school history for several years before finally landing her first newspaper job. After her marriage to Burt, the couple resided in Texas for several more years, working at papers in Fort Worth, Dallas, Houston, and San Antonio. Between 1923 and 1925 Clare lived apart from Burt in Europe, reporting for Texas papers on international events. It was said she was the last reporter to interview novelist Joseph Conrad before his death.

In 1925 Clare returned to Texas to become press secretary for Miriam A. (Ma) Ferguson, Texas' controversial first woman governor. Meanwhile Burt that same year was hired by the New York *Morning Herald* to serve as the paper's drama editor and critic and work as a press agent for showman Florenz Ziegfeld of Ziegfeld Follies fame. Miriam left her press secretary post to join him in 1926, three years later drawing on her experiences with Ma Ferguson to publish a novel, *The Woman of It*, about—surprise—a woman governor of a southern state.

Having caught the fiction bug, Clare collaborated with John over the next four years on four novels, three of which were mysteries, which were then enjoying a terrific vogue in the United States, with S. S. Van Dine's critically lauded Philo Vance puzzlers ascending high up on the bestseller charts, inspiring hosts of hopeful imitators. Clare and John were no slavish followers of the Great Detective school of mystery, however. To the contrary,

their mysteries were models of what was then deemed real-
ism, with protagonists who are ordinary onlookers as well
as amateur sleuths, helping the police solve the crimes
but being by no means showoff, tediously declamatory
geniuses like hoity-toity Philo Vance and Lord Peter Wim-
sey. Clearly the couple brought their own extensive professional portfolios to bear on their crime writing.

In *Smoke Screen*, the debut Lawrence Saunders detective novel, the protagonist surely not altogether coinciden-
tally is a daring woman newspaper reporter in Houston,
Texas. A "keen-witted society girl" bored with teas and
dances who fervently desires to be taken seriously at the
male-dominated *Pioneer*, Sally Lomax is returning from a
roadhouse early one morning with Johnny Rorke, hotshot
star of the staff, when a fire engine shrieks by them. Sally
insists to the jaded Johnny that they pursue the vehicle.
"Sally always followed fire engines," we are told, hoping
to find a hot story. This time the one she and Johnny dis-
cover is a five-alarm scorcher!

In the smoldering remains of a partially burnt bunga-
low are found the bodies of an old man and a pretty young
woman—and it soon becomes apparent, in part due to
Sally's pertinacious on-the-spot investigating, that the
fire was deliberately set and its victims actually murdered.
Sally has finally found her big story and no one is going
to deflect "Miss Sherlock" from chasing it, no matter how
much the danger heats up! At first she is treated patron-
izingly by her colleagues, but eventually her editor, Andy
Hunt, is upbraiding himself for his male chauvinism: "By
God, he had taken this girl for a society dumb-bell! Wanted to fire her! Suppose he had! Good Lord!"

Granted, Sally enjoys every social advantage in life—she
has not only a devoted black maid, Lulu, but her brother,
Dick, happens to be Houston's DA—but she is not afraid

to get her dainty hands dirty. And dirty is just what this double murder case turns out to be before truth eventually is outed. "[T]hat was the way the game was played," thinks Sally unsentimentally when it is all over. "She had been a sneak and an eavesdropper and felt proud of herself."

One suspects that *Smoke Screen* was written mostly by Clare and that the follow-up Lawrence Saunders mystery, *The Columnist Murder*, came more from Burt's hand. In this book a corpse is discovered shot in a phone booth during the debut performance of a hit show at the New Netherland Theater on Broadway. The victim is newspaper society gossip columnist Tommy Twitchell, whom the authors obviously based upon real-life society gossip columnist Walter Winchell (1897-1972), who a couple years earlier in 1929, while working at the *New York Daily Mirror*, had inaugurated the country's first syndicated gossip column, *On Broadway*.

Tommy Twitchell's dead body is discovered by youthful native Norwegian Nels Lundberg, the house fireman on duty at the theater, whom the authors describe as "[t]wenty-five, blond, burly and handsome" and one reviewer praised for his "Scandinavian phlegm." Nels fervently desires to become a cop and manages to tag along for the police investigation into Tommy's murder, which concludes about eight hours later. Nels makes some important discoveries himself, like the torn copy of Tommy's latest innuendo-laden column (facsimile copies of which were included in the original hardcover edition of the detective novel). Can the motive for Tommy's murder be found in a fatal, final divulgement of tittle-tattle from the gossip writer?

The authors dedicated *The Columnist Murder* to Walter Winchell, who certainly had nothing to take umbrage with in the book concerning tittle-tattle about himself.

A Columnist's Sec'y Jots Down a Few Notes

Dear W. W.: I saw a sample jacket of "The Columnist Murder," the crime novel which Farrar-Rinehart plan to present in July...It is a striking cover for a book, revealing a blood-stained finger pointing to an item such as appears in your quidnunc col'm...A blurb states: "A gossip item looked harmless, but three gruesome deaths followed!"...Have yourself a shiver...They say, however, that Lawrence Saunders (Burton Davis to you!) has done a thrilling job of it, but so far as I am concerned he will go down in literary history as being another novelist who turned yellow when it came to mentioning your name, when he meant you...

He calls his central character "Tommy Twitchell" . . . How subtle! . . . At any rate, this is the book in which you are killed while in a phone booth during a performance of the "Follies" . . . By the way, Time, the magazine, phoned . . . Wanted to know if the time had not expired on the statement of six months ago in Zit's Weekly that you would be bumped off within six months . . . As soon as you come in rush upstairs to Mr. K . . . What have you done now?

1931

Although by the 1960s Winchell—who had distinguished himself in the McCarthyite Fifties as a notorious McCarthyite redbaiter and cruelly wanton career destroyer—was generally despised, at the inception of his career in the early Thirties he was tolerated rather more as a playful scamp. I happen to have a copy of the novel that contains an inscription from Burt and Clare to Robert John Conway, *who helped a lot.* Robert John Conway (1899-1972) was a nationally prominent journalist who had covered the infamous Hall-Mills and Snyder-Gray murder trials in 1926 and 1927 respectively. He would go on to receive a nomination for a Pulitzer Prize in 1935 for his coverage of the Bruno Hauptman Lindbergh baby kidnapping trial.

In 1932 Burton and Clare Ogden Davis published a final detective novel, *Devil's Den*, which they set in the Devil's Den Preserve, the largest natural park in southwestern Connecticut and one of the biggest in the metropolitan New York area. Nels Lundberg, now a cop, is again on a case in this, the last and by far the longest of the Lawrence Saunders detective novels. Hopefully it too will be reprinted someday.

To

CHARLOTTE BARBOUR

We kiss your hand, madame!

1

Sally always followed fire engines. She swung the car expertly to the right onto Telephone Road, planted a suede pump firmly on the foot throttle and watched the speedometer crawl up to fifty, sixty. The sirens were hooting and howling off to the northwest as the canary-colored roadster raced through a colony of bungalows dotted along the prairie toward the distant, dismal din. Closer together the houses flashed by, as the car hummed angrily along the concrete in the darkness.

"The haunts of vice and crime weren't so hot, Johnny," she complained to the man at her side. "Perhaps this will be hotter."

"I didn't take you to the worst places," Johnny countered wearily. "What's more, I won't. But you wanted to see the roadhouses, and you saw four of them. What did you expect—a bucket of blood? You saw a lot of cheap drunks, you put quarters in the pianos, you danced around with a lot of white trash, and drank a little corn. You've seen life; now you can go home and dream about it."

"I'm not going home," said Sally, grinning. "I'm going to a fire. If you don't like it, you can walk home."

"I'm powerful sleepy, but I'm kind to children and dumb animals," Johnny softened. "I hope it's a good fire, if that will satisfy you."

He looked at her quizzically. A good gal this, for all her society upbringing and her spoiled darling background; of no use in a newspaper office, but a good sort, and highly ornamental. If she wanted to play at being a reporter, let her play. She'd tire of it in a few weeks and go gallivanting off in search of new sensations. If he had as much money as Sally Lomax had, with no strings tied to it, he'd go to Afghanistan and Africa and the Island of Bali and on through the alphabet of adventure. Hello! What's that? An airplane—roaring across the road ahead, just missing the telephone wires.

The fire sirens, racing in from three directions, were coming to a focus close ahead, but there was no sign of a blaze. Up the road, headlights flared. Sally slowed and stopped the car.

"You know enough to park out of their way," Johnny approved.

"I'm the well-trained fire fan," she said. "Let's walk up and see the pretty engines."

"I'm not willing, but I'm weak," Johnny grumbled, getting out slowly. "I don't believe there is a fire."

"Yes, there is," insisted Sally. "I smell it. Funny there's no blaze showing." She was hurrying as fast as high heels would permit.

"Did you see an airplane?" she asked, suddenly.

"Yes."

"Good. I thought maybe I was dreaming." A motor pumper howled past them to a fire plug, backed and turned and overtook them, spinning out a flat ribbon of hose like toothpaste from a tube. They picked their way between red trucks and running rubber coats, until they came to the center of all this fantastic fury. Two searchlights flooded the facade of a shabby two-story residence, relic of an older and more spacious day in a section since dedicated to variegated villas and bright, banal bungalows. Bath-robed and slippered men, women in coats over nightgowns, excited children, clustered chattering in the road and on lawns and porches.

An ax whacked expertly at the front door of the blear-eyed old ruin. Pike poles ripped through window frames; glass shivered; hose lines spat white water and bored into black clouds that poured through the breached door and windows. Red flame flared up in the eyes of the monster, yellow flashes shot through the smoke. This was a pretty good fire, after all; it had only needed air. But half a dozen white rods of water were now beating down the flames, firemen were swarming up ladders to attack the beast from above; slowly they were snuffing it.

Ten minutes later Johnny was following an assistant chief's white helmet through the front door. Inside were still smoke and smolder and the sharp stench of wet, charred wood.

"Hello, Rorke," bellowed the chief, turning his flashlight into Johnny's eyes. "You got here quick."

"Out joy-riding," said Johnny. "Anybody live here?"

"Empty, I reckon," said the chief, flashing his light around. "Just as well it burned. Old fire trap . . . hell-o!" The flashlight had picked out a queer long mass on the floor. Johnny strode across and bent over it. He straightened and looked up at the chief, and then back at the blackened bundle.

"Hey! Inside, here!" The chief's great voice boomed. "Where's Ben Hosey?" He turned his flashlight on a rubber coat swishing and thumping in through the door. "Get them lanterns! Hurry up! They's a body in here! Get one of them motor cops to call in and get an ambulance and a justice of the peace out here. Tell 'em there's a feller burned up."

Half a dozen firemen clumped in, two with bright lanterns.

"We'll have a look around," said the chief to Johnny. "May be somebody else in here. That feller is sure cooked; right in the heart of the fire. Bill, you take a couple of boys and go through upstairs. Go up the ladders; that staircase is out."

The chief made another circuit of the room. It appeared to be a living-room, with the staircase running up the right and rear walls. There was the wire skeleton of a couch bed over against the rear wall under the stairs, a couple of charred pine chairs, a heavy mission table in the center of the room. The body lay between the couch and the table, on its back. It was a man's body; that was all Johnny had been able to tell.

The chief clumped across and opened a door at the rear of the living-room, next the lefthand wall. Johnny followed. This was the kitchen; a gas stove, a pine table, four chairs and a cheap refrigerator its only furnishings, blackened but unburned. The back door was locked, but there was no key in it. Through a door at their left, they passed into a room bare of furniture except for a canvas army cot, spread with blankets, and one chair. This had been, in the heyday of the house, the dining-room, Johnny decided. The door connecting it with a room at the front of the house was locked, but the key was in it. The chief unlocked it, and Johnny followed him through. The light from the lantern glinted on a smoke-begrimed brass bedstead, scorched sheets and blankets tousled upon it.

There was carpet on the floor; a chair near the head of the bed, a marble-topped washstand with a bowl and pitcher were revealed as the flashlight swung around. On the bed, across the foot, something furry crouched or huddled. The two men stopped still.

"A woman," said Johnny, clearing his throat. He went near to her.

A woman it was, in a gray squirrel coat, her red-gold hair showing beneath a cloche hat of black felt. The face was scorched, the hair and the fur coat singed and curled by the heat. Apparently she had been asphyxiated.

"Why in hell didn't she open the window and jump out?" asked the chief, standing open-mouthed over this second victim in what had been "an empty shack." "It ain't burned bad in here and she must have had time."

He tried to open the window; he couldn't budge it. He played his flashlight around the inside of the frame and fumbled at the side of the sash.

"It was locked with a spike through a hole bored in the sash," he explained to Johnny, exhibiting a heavy nail. "I reckon she didn't know that."

"She couldn't get through the dining-room because that door was locked on the other side," Johnny reasoned. "The fire started out there where we found the man. She ran in here and was trapped." He looked around. The door into the living-room was closed, but its lower panels were burned through. He tried it; it swung open.

"Well, we've got to leave everything lay as it is until the justice gets here for the inquest," said the chief. "Suppose we go outside and get some air. It don't smell too good to me."

"Beyond the scent of your roasted friend in here," said Johnny, sniffing as they went into the living-room, "I think I can smell oil . . . yeah, it smells like . . . by golly, like kerosene."

"Let's have a look," said the chief.

It took a bare minute for the two, with the flashlight and a fireman's lantern, to find on the floor the burner of a kerosene lamp and scattered fragments of heavy glass, pieces of the base and bowl of the lamp.

"Look here," called the chief, suddenly, "the key's broke off in this front door lock. Right flush with the keyhole." He played the light on the floor. "Here's the shank of it, too," he added, stooping to pick it up.

"There's the whole story," said Johnny. "The lamp on this center table was knocked over. The man tried to smother it; the lamp exploded; he tried to unlock the front door; it was jammed; he broke off the key, like a crazy man. The girl had run into the bedroom. She was trapped and smothered to death. Now, if we get them identified, I'll be all set to put out an extra by seven o'clock in the morning. Let's go talk to the neighbors and see if we can find out who they were."

"Hey, I've got a fire department to run, young feller!"

Johnny grinned and trailed after the chief, out the front door. At the gate in the old picket fence a girl in a fur-trimmed coat, bareheaded, was arguing with a motor-cycle policeman and all but crying with repressed rage. It was Sally Lomax.

"Hey, there!" called Johnny, hurrying to her. "I forgot all about you. What's the trouble?"

"This officer wouldn't let me go into the house. He wouldn't believe I was a reporter and had a perfect right to go in. I haven't my police card with me."

"She didn't look like a reporter to me, but if she's with you, Mister Rorke, and you won't let her get hurt, it's all right with me." The man in olive drab touched his cap and stepped back.

"You don't want to go in there," said Johnny, earnestly. "There's a couple of dead people, and one of them's too well roasted. It's not pretty."

"If I'm going to be a reporter," Sally protested, "I can't be squeamish."

"If you want to be of some use as a reporter," snapped Johnny, "you'll help me ask the neighbors who this man and woman were. That's the important thing right now."

He moved off. Sally meekly followed.

No neighbor could be found who knew much about the occupants of the house. An old man lived there; no one knew his name. He drove a dilapidated car. He had lived there more than a year; one man said nearly two years. He remained a mystery, however long it had been. He had occasional callers, at odd hours of the night, always in automobiles, sometimes in big costly cars. The shades were drawn down, day and night. He bothered no one. He would speak when spoken to, but he wouldn't talk two minutes and nothing could be got out of him. They didn't know who owned the house; some lawyer had bought the property a couple of years back. He had laid out those gravel streets. Nice piece of ground, even if the house was worth next to nothing. The old guy might be a bootlegger, one man thought, though there was nothing to make you believe it except those big cars that came at night.

The plot of ground on which the house stood was an extensive holding. Two wide graveled streets cut through the tract at right angles, and the house stood in one corner of their intersection, a block south of Telephone Road. The nearest neighbors lived two blocks away, in either direction along the Road.

Sally was reporting her meager list of findings to Johnny, when the justice of the peace, who in Texas acts as coroner, arrived. They followed him into the house. Johnny knelt beside the dead man, alongside the justice; Sally took one good look and retreated to the door. She was, after all, not needed at the moment and it was close in the room.

But Johnny was not squeamish.

"Let's see if there is anything under him," he said. A fireman rolled the body over. There was an old leather bill fold, charred at one end, in an unburned patch of trouser cloth. Johnny went over to a lantern standing on the lower step of the burned stairway and examined the wallet. Sally, watching him from the doorway, saw him tuck a little slip of paper into his vest pocket, after a quick look around, and turn back to the justice of the peace and the fire chief.

"Well, this guy had a little money, Judge," he remarked. "Look here."

The justice took the charred bills and counted. "Ten, twenty, one, two, three, four—twenty-four dollars. Numbers here; it's still good. Nothing else. No name on the purse, nothing else in it. Can't tell much about how he looked. Two lower front teeth gone. Well, well! Where's the other body?"

The chief led the way, and Johnny and the justice, followed by a fireman with a lantern, went into the bedroom. The justice stood at the foot of the bed, studying the body; he leaned over closer and turned it. Between the woman's knee and the dirty sheet, they found a beaded bag. The justice opened it; there were a dozen keys on a silver ring, a twenty-dollar note, ninety-two cents, a silver vanity case, a lace-edged handkerchief. Nothing with a name on it.

As they stood there, staring down at the body, a muffled squeak behind them whirled them around. Transfixed in the circle of the chief's flashlight, stood Sally.

"Johnny! I know that woman!" she blurted.

"You do?"

"Who is she?"

"Alice Blair. She has a dress shop on South Main."

"Wait, Sally! Are you sure?"

"I think so." She edged a little closer, peering down. "It looks exactly like her, and she has red hair, but the face is a little fat for her."

"That's from the heat, Miss Sally," the justice explained.

"Ready to move this body, Judge?" Two ambulance men with a stretcher had come in. The justice nodded, and Sally again fled to the front porch. Behind the stretcher-bearers as they came out, was Johnny.

"You may be of some use after all, kid," he said, cheerily, to the pale girl. "Let's get to a telephone and call this Blair girl's house. Do you know where she lives?"

"Yes. Over her shop."

"Well, that's easy. There's a telephone in that first house down the road. Come along."

Sally's hands trembled as they thumbed the telephone book, looking down the line of B's. Blair, Miss Alice, Modes, 3502 South Main Boulevard; Blair, Miss Alice, r 3502 South Main Boulevard, Hadley 3863. Johnny called the number. Sally could hear the buzz as the operator rang again and again.

"Hadley thrrree-eight-six-thrrree does not answer."

"It's four-thirty," said Rorke, as he hung up the receiver. "I don't think we can get much more out here; let's go to the Blair place and see if we can rouse anybody there."

While Sally was driving across Polk Avenue toward South Main, she searched her memory for all she knew of Alice Blair. She had known the modiste for nearly two years, and had bought several dresses and some underwear at her shop.

"I think she must be about twenty-five years old. She's very pretty," she told Rorke. "Red hair with brown eyes; unusual, you know; red-headed women nearly always have gray eyes or blue. She lived in Paris for some time, and she does know—did know—good clothes. She has had this shop as long as I've known her; I met her just after she opened it. She has done pretty well with it, I think."

"Know anything about her reputation?"

"I never heard a word against her. She was one of those gentle, calm girls; well poised and well educated. She was born somewhere here in Texas; she told me where, once, but I've forgotten. I don't believe she had ever been married; at least, I always thought of her as unmarried."

She stopped the car in front of an arcade apartment of Spanish Colonial design. A street light on the corner showed the wide-arched windows of the first-floor shops; on the second from the corner small black letters modestly advised the passer-by: Alice Blair, Importer, Modes, Lingerie.

Rorke and Sally peered into the shop. The single light showed neat cases and cabinets, shrouded for the night in gay, glazed chintzes.

They went into the entrance to the building, off which the shop door also opened. One letter box and doorbell slab were labeled "Blair." Johnny thumbed the bell button. They could hear its buzz overhead, faintly. He rang steadily for a minute, then again. Neither he nor Sally spoke as they turned back to the car at the curb. Just as they reached it, a motorcycle screeched to a stop; a policeman dismounted.

"Hey, Pete!" Johnny called.

"Hello, Johnny! What you doing here?"

"Stopped to see about the Blair woman? She's not there. We just tried."

"No? Well, I'll just give her another ring." They waited while he clumped up to the door and entered the vestibule. Presently he returned, saying, "I guess it's her all right." He mounted and rode off.

Sally drove slowly toward town. When she spoke, it was in a small, subdued voice.

"That's terrible, Johnny." The tragedy was beginning to be real to her.

"Stop at Mike Genora's, Sally. Let's have some coffee." Johnny was not unkind, but he was too busy thinking to talk much now. Sally kept silent. She had never been out on a big story before, and she wanted, desperately, not to appear to be too much of a cub.

Rorke was her current hero. She was proud of his approval, though she suspected it was approval of her sportsmanship and sturdy spirit, rather than a belief that she would ever be the "newspaper man" he had promised to try to make her. Rorke had been a reporter since before the war. Tall, lean, ugly enough to make women think him fascinating, his gray eyes had already seen too much of life's petty dramas.

As he would have expressed it, he was no longer given to "taking any wooden nickels." He was interested in Sally Lomax as a new specimen; she amused him, and her adoration of his superior knowledge flattered him. Lazy and energetic by turns, he was deeply in love with his work, although he swore intermittently that he was "bored as hell with all of it." He talked, customarily, like that; at heart, he said, he was a "forty-dollar flatfoot," but he could write like an archangel playing on human heartstrings when he wanted to.

He was, Sally had some time ago decided, a gentleman by birth, but a newspaperman by choice. His taste in tailors she admired. In the office he smoked a pipe with a heavenly stink; he always smelled of good tobacco. She knew little else about him, except that he came from Georgia—a place called Rome—and had studied at some vague, small college, leaving untimely to turn reporter in New Orleans. He had come to Houston late in 1917 for air service training; kept there as an instructor at Ellington Field, he had liked the place well enough to stay after he was discharged from the service. He had applied to the *Pioneer* for a job; he was now the town's top reporter.

His efforts to "make a newspaperman of Sally Lomax" were condoned by the rest of the staff as one of the star reporter's temporary sentimental flurries. The city editor had told Rorke he was wasting the *Pioneer's* time. Andy Hunt, nominally city editor and actually managing editor

of the paper—for the managing editor was at Mineral Wells
laving his rheumatism—was plainly bored with Sally.

A newspaperman for thirty years, Hunt had no interest
beyond his paper. He gave to it what he demanded from
his staff, the utmost in devoted effort each day. There are
newspapers scattered all across the country that owe their
vitality to the Andy Hunts who direct them. There are fat
Hunts and slim Hunts, honest Hunts and rascals; all of
them are persons to be reckoned with: good editors, sometimes great editors. It just happened that the one in charge
of the *Houston Pioneer* was honest, and, at bottom, kindly.
His good temper had long since vanished in the wake of
lazy reporters and self-seeking, spineless or stubborn own-
ers of the papers he had run.

His hair was iron gray; to see him with a coat on and
his hat off was unusual. Short, wiry, of indefinite age, he
was a dynamo of nerves and energy. Society girls who had
wormed their way into his staffs he had had to endure before, here and there. Only the fact that this one's brother
was Richard Lomax, born to wealth, influence and social
standing, become district attorney of Harris County, kept
Hunt from firing Sally over the publisher's head. A realist
always, he hoped some day to have use for this girl's connections.

Not that Lomax wanted his sister to be a reporter. He
had tried objections, overruled; a mandate, defied; ridi-
cule, ignored. Sally had stayed on the *Pioneer,* doing those
picayunish jobs every one in an editorial room hates;
writing obituary notices, covering women's clubs and lun-
cheons, unimportant school board meetings; answering
the telephone for busy and important reporters, and hun-
gering for something real. She had read fiction about cub
reporters; they always made good dramatically and con-
founded the superior veterans, who thereupon admitted

the cub to full fellowship in the mystic order of printer's ink. She still half believed those yarns.

She was an attractive, healthy twenty-two, confident but not forward, well-bred, a State University graduate. Tall, slender, she carried herself with hard-muscled grace. Her dark brown hair in an unruly bob topped an eager, intelligent face; her brown eyes more often sparkled with humor than softened with feminine guile.

She had been early advised by a salty old editorial writer that no good reporter talked too much. She recalled that axiom this morning, following Johnny meekly into the all-night restaurant, and perching on a high stool at the counter. Dumbly she drank coffee, and motioned casually to the waiter for more. Johnny finished his own second cup. They went back to the car. Not a word had been exchanged for ten minutes.

"Let's drive by Westheimer's," he suggested. "The boys may have found something on one of those bodies by this time."

She stayed in the car in front of the undertaker's place, adjoining police headquarters, while Rorke went in. In a few minutes he returned, lighting a cigar.

"You may be right, kid." He stood with one foot on the running board of the car. "That girl's underwear is very fine stuff, and all of it has 'A. B.' embroidered on it. And her eyes are brown." Sally's hands tightened on the wheel; she smiled, though nervously, at Rorke.

"Well, youngster, let's get to the office. It's five o'clock. Time to wake up the old man and the crew for an extra."

"Is there anything I can write, Johnny?"

"Sure there is. You can write plenty, for once in your life." He grinned at her. "Likely this is your great chance, Sally. You talked to the woman who discovered the fire. And you know all we know about the Blair girl. Andy will want you to write a story about her—maybe a sob story.

Keep it simple; don't try to sob. Don't use any sad adjectives, but make 'em read it and weep."

Sally labored harder during the next hour and a half than she had ever toiled at anything before. It was flattering to be ordered about by Mr. Hunt, like a real reporter instead of an intruder to whom he must be civil. It was thrilling to see in print the first story she had ever written for the front page, changed and chopped, but still hers.

Daylight was full on when the first copies of the extra came up to the city room. She lighted the cigarette Mr. Hunt had offered her casually, and read the damp print lovingly. Presently she pulled out a slide of her battered desk and cocked her feet up on it. The cut steel buckles on her soggy suede slippers winked at her. She blew a thin, reflective column of cheap cigarette smoke at them, and flipped the butt into the middle of the floor: a reporter at last.

2

Johnny Rorke sauntered over.

"Tired, kid?" he asked. "Want to run me out to the house again?"

"Yes. What do you want to go back for?"

"Oh, just to see what we can see in daylight. I want to look at that lamp again. . . . Damn' funny why that woman didn't go out the back door instead of into that bedroom. . . . But that back door was locked and no key in it." He was thinking aloud, while Sally was putting on her coat.

A hundred assorted folk were buzzing around the place as Sally stopped the car in front of the burned house. A policeman standing guard at the front gate spoke to Rorke and touched his cap to Sally.

They looked first at the spot where the body of the man had lain. The threadbare carpet under him had not been burned, though it was wet and stained.

"Well, one thing stands out," said Johnny jovially. "There's not going to be much insurance collected on the furniture in this place. Must have cost all of thirty dollars when it was new—which was years and years ago. Let's look at the bedroom."

Sally, ahead of him, sniffed as she went in.

"Funny how that kerosene smell stays, isn't it?"

"Sure is. Seems to me to be stronger in here than it is out there."

"Johnny, look at this carpet!"

Soaked with water, black with char washed in by the hose streams, it shone iridescent with oil in the daylight.

Johnny crouched on his heels and rubbed the carpet with his fingers; held them to his nose. Like a couple of pups, they sniffed around the floor, stood up and gazed solemnly at each other.

"Kerosene in this carpet." Sally pronounced a dictum.

"Nothing but, kid, nothing but. This gets thicker and thicker." Rorke bent over and smelled the wet and grimy bed covers. "Same here. Plenty. Let's look around. There's something more than an accident in this."

They passed through the "dining-room" into the drab and dirty kitchen.

"There were whiskey glasses on the table in here," Johnny remarked. "The fire marshal took 'em down with him. I said in my story that the old man and the girl had got drunk and turned the lamp over. I'm revising that brilliant decision rapidly. How could one quart of oil spread through two rooms and up on that bed?"

He opened the door onto the little back porch; the door had been unlocked, evidently, by a fireman's skeleton key. There, glistening in the first rays of the sun coming through the distant pine trees, stood a five-gallon oil can of galvanized tin. It was back against the wall, where it would not have been easily picked out by a fireman's lantern. Rorke unscrewed the cap, then picked up the can, glitteringly new.

"Hot dog," he whispered to himself. "Look at this!" he called back to the girl, who was still lingering in the dingy kitchen. "You wanted crime last night. You got it!"

"How, Johnny?"

"That, little one, is a five-gallon can. It has been full of kerosene. It has been full of kerosene quite recently; in fact, it has been put down here recently, which is more to the point. If you don't believe it, look on the porch. That greasy ring is where the can stood, full enough to slop over. It's empty now. Who emptied it inside there? And why?"

"Oh!" Sally's wondering voice sounded very, very young.

"Um . . . Doesn't look now like just a lamp exploded, does it? No, ma'am!"

He leaped off the porch and hurried around toward the front of the house, to bring the policeman back with him.

"Around here, Morgan. Look at that can, will you?"

"Say, that's funny!" said the bluecoat, picking up the can and setting it down, reflectively.

"Well, unusual, anyway, Morgan. Say, what's upstairs in this shack?"

"Ain't nothin'. Them rooms up there's as bare as a bone."

"Naw?"

"Surest thing you know, Mr. Rorke. Want to climb up that ladder and look?"

Johnny was coming down the ladder from a fruitless inspection of bare and blackened walls and roof, when he heard Sally call him from inside the house. He traced her voice to the closet under the stairway. A mass of crumpled newspaper came flying out to him, followed by another bundle; after them came Sally, face smudged, hands grimy.

"It's all filled with newspapers, just soaked with kerosene," she said breathlessly. "Johnny, they wanted everything in this house to burn up!"

"You don't say! You're getting smarter and smarter, Miss Sherlock!" He patted her grimy cheek. "Come on, let's get to a telephone. The old man is going to grab this arson angle. Besides, I want to get down to the post-office as soon as it opens." He kicked the loose papers back into the closet and closed the door.

"Why do you want to go to the post-office?" she asked, as she started the car.

"Business. Step on it, honey. Say, who owned that house? Didn't I hear you telling the old man? And don't take that next corner so fast, will you? I'm in a hurry, but not to be killed. I know too much."

"Bob Morrison owns that whole tract. At least the fire marshal said he did."

"Morrison? Well, he won't miss what he lost on that shack. He's got plenty. So much that he craves to waste it running for governor."

"Do you reckon he has a chance? Dick thinks he has, but maybe the wish is father to the thought. He helped Dick a lot getting elected, you know, and they are thicker than thieves. I thought maybe Dick just wanted him elected so much that he wouldn't believe anything else."

"Too far ahead of the primaries to tell. I've sorter thought the Judge's lady friend wanted him to run more than he did. What do you think about that? You know her of course."

"Who, Mrs. Curtis? I don't see why they don't get married and be through with it. But then, I reckon it's his procrastination. He's the laziest-looking skinny man I ever saw. And getting elected is such a lot of fuss and bother."

"Well, I reckon he's going to run. He asked me to take over his publicity on the side. Hey—there's your brother!"

Sally shot her car ahead to draw alongside its twin, a sedate dark green instead of canary. The man in the other roadster pulled over to the curb and stopped.

"Sally Lomax! Where have you been? What are you up to now? Look at your face!" Trying to be stern, her brother was grinning in spite of himself.

"We've been to a fire, Dick. Two people burned up." She tried to make it sound professionally callous. Being the baby sister was an enduring curse; Dick wouldn't take her work seriously.

"Yes? Try to rescue them and get your face that dirty? Go home and wash it." Now he was openly laughing at her.

"No, really, Dick, this is serious. We think the house was set afire."

Lomax turned to Rorke. Johnny's serious face sobered the district attorney at once.

"What's this, Rorke?"

Johnny outlined, briefly, the story, adding the clews he and Sally had just uncovered. Lomax, who had listened in silence, stepped on the starter of his car.

"Thanks, Rorke. The morning paper didn't have it. I'll see what they know at my office. Sally, you'd better go home and wash your face." His car shot forward.

Sally made a face at his back, and turned to Johnny.

"Where to, now?"

"Nearest telephone, a beanery, and the post-office. I'll buy you some breakfast, young woman, if you'll go home and wash your face, as your brother told you to. You aren't as pretty as you could be. Reckon I'm not, either."

Sally left him at a drugstore near the post-office, and drove home, declining his breakfast invitation. At nine-thirty she was back in the *Pioneer* office, reading the made-over extra, bannered *"Two Die in Arson Plot Blaze."* Andy Hunt was no piker.

John Rorke's story on the front page revealed that the dead man was Martin Fox, said to have been about sixty years old, identified through a half-charred postal money order receipt. (Rorke didn't tell how he had pocketed this when he had opened the dead man's half-burned bill fold.) The stub had shown only the first three numbers 976—,

the amount, $92, and part of the stamp of the issuing
office, Houston, Feb. —; the rest of the date was charred
off. The post-office clerk's book had shown that one Martin Fox had sent a money order for ninety-two dollars to
a banker in Longleaf, Texas, on February third. The clerk
recalled that Fox had been sending approximately a hundred dollars to that bank every month for a year and a
half; every clerk in the money order department had come
to know the old man.

Rorke's story went on to relate that a reporter had talked to the cashier of the Longleaf State Bank as soon as this
had been learned.

> "Martin Fox was born near Longleaf, and lived
> here until about fifteen years ago," the banker
> had said. "He left here to go to Dallas, and
> moved from there to Houston more than two
> years ago. He has been buying a small farm
> near Longleaf, where a tenant is raising hogs
> for him on shares. He bought the farm three
> years ago and started paying it out in small
> monthly payments. About two years ago, after
> he went to Houston, he raised the amount he
> paid to around a hundred dollars a month. He
> always remitted by postal money order.

> "I don't know what he worked at in Hous-
> ton," (the banker was quoted further). "I am
> under the impression that he was a collector
> for a firm of lawyers. He was always a secre-
> tive sort; once I asked him what he wanted
> with a farm at his age—he must have been
> about sixty—and he said: 'So I won't have to
> keep my money in a bank.' He had no folks
> around here; they all died years ago. He told
> me once he would never marry. Wouldn't be
> bothered with women."

The banker had added that a pair of Martin Fox's lower front teeth were missing; this supported the identification.

The *Pioneer* had made two clean beats so far. Sally felt, a glow of virtuous pride; she had achieved this just by liking to chase fire engines, at which juvenility the uppity Mr. Rorke had been amused. Yet, if she hadn't wanted to see a fire, Alice Blair would not have been identified yet, and Johnny would not have had the money order stub that had identified old Fox. The *Evening Record* and the *Morning Bulletin* were left far behind, thanks to her. The *Record* had put out an extra, but it was only an echo of the *Pioneer's*.

The later *Pioneer* had merely added to Sally's first story of Alice Blair the fact that her employees at the shop had not been found for questioning. The fire stories all but filled the front page, surrounding a double column "box" in boldface type:

Alice Blair, about 25, red-haired beauty, and Martin Fox, about 60, at 2:30 a.m. today were burned to death in an old house on Telephone Road, just outside the city limits.

Who Was Alice Blair?
Why Was She Alone in the House with Fox?
Who Soaked the Premises with
Kerosene and Set the Fire?
Why Didn't the Man and the Woman Escape?

Read the *Houston Pioneer*
for answers to these questions.
The News while it *IS* News.
Crisp Correct Complete

3

Andy Hunt noticed Sally at her desk in the far corner of the city room, just as she finished reading the revised extra. "Sally!" The city editor bawled it across the long, dingy room. Sally's heart gave a little leap. Mr. Hunt was accepting her. Maybe those cub reporter romances did come true, sometimes! He had never called her anything but a wry "Miss Lomax" before. She hurried to his desk.

"Go out to the Blair shop and see what you can get out of the girls who work there. Find out where this girl came from and where her folks are. I've got young Havens out there, but he's dead or something. Get a picture of her. Phone in as soon as you get anything. Noon edition dead line is ten-thirty, remember." He might have been giving orders to a star reporter, Sally thought.

"Get art!" He yelled after her. Sally giggled. Calling cheap photographs "art" was to her the "funniest gag in the newspaper racket," putting it professionally.

She spent the next half hour at the shop, talking to two tearful young saleswomen, discovering exactly nothing about Alice Blair's past. They didn't know one thing about her; she had spoken, vaguely, of a sister, but they didn't know where the sister lived, or even her name. Miss Blair had been in the shop all of the day before; a representative of a New York importing house had been there for the past three days and Miss Blair had been occupied with this woman. She was an old acquaintance of Miss Blair's, or at least she had seemed to be; they called each other "Alice" and "Grace." Miss Blair had said, when they closed up last night, that she wouldn't be at the shop to-day until some time after noon.

They had no key to the apartment upstairs. They had no photograph of Miss Blair. She hadn't been easy to get intimate with. Always very nice, and very kindly, too, but reserved. Neither of them had ever heard her speak of any Martin Fox; they had never heard her talk to him over the telephone; once in a while she talked to a man whom she called "Terry." They didn't know Terry's last name. She never called him; always he phoned her. They had never heard her mention any other man, except on business.

Miss Blair didn't drink? All Sally got for that question was a pair of glares. Certainly she didn't drink! Didn't Miss Lomax know the type of clients Miss Blair had?

"Well, somebody had been drinking whiskey from two glasses out there last night," Sally said. "Why didn't she run out that back door instead of stupidly staying in a room with locked doors and nailed-down windows if she wasn't befuddled with whiskey?"

The younger girl burst into tears, and the older announced that she was going to lock up shop and go home. Sally apologized; she hadn't meant to blacken Miss Blair's memory at all. The girls were still resentful as they put on their hats and coats.

Baffled, Sally drove back to the office. She met Rorke in the lobby, vibrant with his own brand of excitement. She followed at his heels as he dashed into the city room, and yelled at Andy that he had "swell new dope. Shooting it fast." He and Hunt conferred earnestly at Rorke's desk before Johnny started a drumfire on his typewriter.

Rorke had been sitting in an anteroom of the district attorney's office when Benny Riskin, a lawyer, whom he knew as a specialist in credit collections, had come in. Johnny had heard him tell an assistant district attorney that he knew Martin Fox. Johnny, with a wink at the assistant, had whisked the lawyer into the rotunda for a private inquisition.

Riskin had employed Martin Fox for the past two years as a collector. That morning was the first time since Fox had been in his employ that the old man had not been at the office when Riskin arrived. Riskin had been wondering if he might be ill, when the *Pioneer's* extra, identifying the burned man, had been brought in. The attorney had gone by the undertaker's, where he had made sure the identification was correct, and then had decided that he had better come to the district attorney and tell what he knew of the old man, which was not much.

"Where did Fox live?" Rorke asked.

"He told me when I hired him that he was caretaker of an old house out on Telephone Road somewhere. It was quite a ways from bus and car lines. He had an old ramshackle car he drove around in."

"Made pretty good money, didn't he?"

"I reckon he averaged about twenty-five or thirty dollars a week," Riskin replied. "He wasn't a star collector, but he didn't mind going back time and again to bum accounts; it never seemed to make any difference to him if he got insulted. You couldn't be friendly with him, but I got so I felt sorry for the old man. He didn't have a chick or a child."

"Well, much obliged, Riskin. You'd better tell Lomax all of that." He was headed for a telephone when a hearty voice hailed him.

"Johnny, how are you?"

"Good morning, Judge! What's your business up here?" Rorke turned to shake hands cordially with Robert E. Lee

Morrison, former judge of one of the Houston district courts, eligible bachelor, attorney for the *Pioneer,* prospective candidate for the gubernatorial nomination in the primaries due that summer, who had just come out of the elevator. Johnny fell into step with him as he walked towards Lomax's office.

"I came up to tell Dick what I know about Martin Fox," Morrison said. "That was my old shack that was burned up, you know."

Rorke cast a fearful glance about the district attorney's anterooms as they went down the passage towards the private office at the end of the suite. Thank God, not a man from the *Record* or *Bulletin* in sight! That was a break! One or another would be there before he got Morrison and Riskin into Lomax's office, if he didn't hurry. But he managed to get the door closed safely behind them.

Lomax welcomed Morrison heartily, shook hands with Riskin, and the four men sat down.

"I was just telling Johnny that I know a few things about Martin Fox," said Morrison. "You know, it was my house that was burned."

"Yes. I had just telephoned to your office, asking you to come over as soon as you could, Bob. Your stenographer said you hadn't come in yet."

"No, I read Johnny's story at breakfast, and drove out there, and then came right on down here, Dick. There isn't a great deal I can tell you about old Martin, though I had known him for years. He used to be a clerk in my firm's offices in Dallas when I was a young lawyer up there. He turned up here about two years ago, saying he had been fired in Dallas, and put up a plea for something to do. I didn't have anything for him to do; he was too old to be of any use in my office. But I hated to turn the old fellow away; he seemed pathetically lonely. I had bought that block of ground out there on Telephone Road as an investment. The house on it was in such bad repair that it couldn't be rented without spending a lot on it, so I just let the old fellow live out there rent free. I loaned him a little money when he first came; about a month later he told me he had a job with Riskin, and began paying back what he borrowed. Now and then he would show up at my office and report the house was all right. There was some insurance on it when he first went out there; I think the policy may be still in force, but I don't know—my secretary attends to that sort of thing. I had told the old man when he first went out there that it was necessary for some one to live in the house to keep the insurance in force. He was a proud old duffer, and I knew it wouldn't do to let him think I was offering him charity."

"Did you ever hear him mention the Blair girl, Judge?" Rorke asked.

"No, that's a queer thing about all this. As long as I knew him in Dallas, I never heard him talk about a woman. I know he never married, or at least I've heard him say he hadn't. What an old codger like that could mean by getting burned up with a pretty girl is beyond me, Dick."

"Did Fox drink?"

"Why, not to speak of, I'd say. I've seen him take a drink up in the Dallas office, years ago, but he wasn't any drunkard, I'm sure."

"I think he had got so he drank a good deal, Judge," put in Riskin. "Every now and then I could smell whiskey on his breath and sometimes he would come into the office with what looked like a bad hangover."

"Well, I shouldn't be surprised; he may have turned into one of these solitary drunkards. Men like that do."

"Did either of you ever hear him speak of his hog farm back in Longleaf?"

Neither Morrison nor Riskin had, they said.

"What I'd like to know is where he got ninety dollars a month to send back there!" Riskin's tone was grim. He repeated to Lomax what he had already told Rorke in the hall.

"Better look over your accounts," advised Lomax. "Could he have been holding out that much money?"

"I don't see how he could have. No collector—and I've had a lot—ever got away with any of *my* money."

All three of his auditors laughed. Riskin, flushing, joined in.

"It must be nice to be a newspaperman—you meet such interesting people!" The trite tag flashed through Rorke's mind as he studied the three men sitting there, talking about the old bill collector. Here were three as diverse as he had seen together in many a day: Lomax, born with the traditional silver spoon in his mouth, the tweeds and pipe, Airedale and sport roadster sort, not brilliant, blustering to cover his lack of keen wit; Morrison, tall, lean, hawk-nosed, handsome, polished, clever for all his lack of driving energy, esteemed a brilliant civil lawyer, cynical, remote, but the devoted friend of the younger district attorney; Riskin, dwarfed, thin, eager, a moth-eaten ferret, worth a good deal of money and hanging onto every penny of it, as tight as his mouth. "Yeah," thought the reporter. "It's a fascinating job. You meet such interesting people! Why in hell do we have to have lawyers, anyway?"

"Well, I'm much obliged to you, Bob, and to you, Riskin, for coming over. If either of you should turn up any other information, or if any one in your offices can supply anything more on Fox, I'll be glad if you'll call me." Lomax dismissed them at the door of his private office.

Rorke parted from the Judge at the courthouse steps. Riskin had hurried off to find out what his bookkeeper could tell about those regular payments to the bank in Longleaf.

The facts disclosed by Judge Morrison and Riskin formed the new elements of the *Pioneer's* late noon edition story on the fire. The few facts that Sally had gathered at the shop were woven into it. The box on the front page asked a new series of questions:

> Where did Fox, earning $25 a week, get $90 to $100 a month to pay on his hog farm?
> Was the dead woman a blackmail victim?
> Why was Fox, a woman-hater, host to such a beautiful young woman?
> Who and where is Alice Blair's sister?
> Who set the house afire and why?

4

At two o'clock that afternoon Johnny Rorke again appeared at the district attorney's office, greeted the waiting *Record* and *Bulletin* men casually, and asked the stenographer in the outer office if Lomax were busy. The man disappeared and presently reported that Lomax wanted to see Rorke at once.

Johnny grinned and went in.

"Look here, Rorke," Lomax snapped before the reporter could close the door, "what do you mean by taking things out of dead men's pockets?"

"Huh? Oh, that money order stub? Why, because I needed it, of course."

"You had no right to touch that body, and you had no right to keep a clew like that from the authorities!"

"What's the matter, Dick? *Record* and *Bulletin* been crawling you?"

Lomax glared.

"I thought they'd get after you about that. Well, that's not your fault. I found that slip, and I kept it. I'm sorry it put you on the pan, but I'd do it again. Perfectly honest about it. Just an old-fashioned reporter, Dick. Only a few of us left." Rorke's eyes twinkled.

"Well, you'll get no more news out of this office—except information that is given to all the press at once." Lomax was genuinely irritated.

"So? I'll give you some news then, if you won't give me any." Johnny placidly lighted a cigarette. "We talked to our correspondent at Longleaf, and what do you think we found out? Alice Blair's history! Yes, sir, we tied little Alice Blair with the red, red hair up with old Martin Fox! Too bad, Dick, the old man's name wasn't Wolf. We could have done a 'Little Red Riding Hood' story."

"You say she was from Longleaf?"

"She was. What's more, her older sister, Angela Blair, was from Longleaf. And Angela had red hair and brown eyes, too."

"Yes?"

"Yes. It seems that Alice left there when she was fourteen, about ten years ago, after her mother died. Angela had been gone for about six years, then; she came back for her mother's funeral and took Alice off with her. No one in Longleaf has heard from them since, so far as our man knows—and he knows it all. There was a rumor that Angela lived here or near here. They had never heard of Alice being in Paris or having a dress shop in Houston."

"It's uncommonly kind of you to bring me the information, Rorke," said Lomax sarcastically.

"We have known all that for two hours. I suppose you're printing it. No chance of your thinking I might want to keep that quiet?"

"That's right; we're printing it. Be in the home edition," he glanced at the office clock, "on the street in twenty minutes, Dick."

"That's a fine break! You've muddled our end of the thing in great style, Rorke!"

"You ought to have called me in and told me what you wanted to keep quiet, Lomax. I might have done it. Can't blame any one but yourself." Johnny sauntered out, enormously at peace with himself and the world. Nice scoop.

Well, he might as well call up Andy and take the rest of the afternoon off. Needed sleep.

Rorke out of the office, Lomax called the *Record,* and asked for George Monroe, the star reporter, disdaining the eager youth waiting outside his door. Monroe, as he admitted sourly, was rewriting the *Pioneer's* fire stories for the home edition, "in a hell of a hurry."

"Well, here, George," Lomax said, "here's some news. If you hustle, you'll beat the *Pioneer*. They have part of it in their home edition, but not all. After this, don't blame me for letting them print news ahead of you. This is protection you're getting now."

He repeated rapidly the story of the Blair sisters' past in Longleaf, adding that his investigators had obtained the information from officers in the little East Texas town, and warning Monroe: "Don't quote me, you understand!"

"Here's something else, too, George: I don't think the dead woman is Alice, after all. It is more likely Angela. The dead woman is more than any twenty-four. I went to Westheimer s and looked at the body, myself. Get this: both

Alice and Angela had red hair and brown eyes, which is more or less unusual. The people in Longleaf said there was a strong resemblance between the little girl, Alice, and her older sister. They must have looked a lot alike as grown women."

"Thanks a lot, Dick. Sure appreciate that. Any idea where Angela lives—or lived?"

"In Galveston. Runs a maternity hospital there under the name of Angela Browning. Perfectly legitimate private hospital; the authorities there have always endorsed it. And, George—Mrs. Browning is missing from the hospital. Hasn't been there since seven o'clock last night. Her staff is worried."

"That's great, Dick. Thanks. We'll spread on this."

Johnny Rorke missed the explosion in the *Pioneer* office when the *Record* home edition hit the street, for Johnny was fast asleep. Andy Hunt had fired only the opening gun of his celebrated battery of profanity, before half a dozen reporters were scurrying to telephones. The bombardment at the city desk continued. Andy himself called Lomax. He gave the district attorney a brisk lesson in sarcastic English that Lomax had to admire while he searched his mind for worthy rejoinders. Lomax's diatribe against Rorke left Andy cold.

"He knew his business," the city editor snapped. "Why didn't you mention some of this to him this morning when he met Morrison and Riskin in your office? You're just mad because something upset you. Now can you tell me anything the *Record* doesn't know?"

"Well, I don't believe any of you know that we have ordered an autopsy on both bodies," Lomax said, politely. "I seem to be conducting this inquiry for the sake of the newspapers. You might as well print that, too."

Hunt ignored the sarcasm. "Thanks; the autopsy story's already in the home edition. Do you know anything more about this Browning woman?"

"No more than the *Record* seems to know."

"Which you told them, of course!" Andy abruptly hung up on the district attorney. A re-write man had called over to him that the Galveston branch office of the *Pioneer* wanted him on another line. Since Galveston and Houston are only fifty miles apart, the newspapers of each city maintain offices in the other.

The *Pioneer's* man in Galveston had to report that Mrs. Browning was well known to the physicians and surgeons of Galveston, as well as to the police and civil authorities. He quoted the chief of police as having said "she was his first thought when his men picked up some forlorn girl, about to become a mother, destitute and desperate," although the chief had hardly phrased it so elegantly. She called her hospital "The Madonna," although it had no connection with any religious body.

"The chief says she always has two or three non-paying patients out there," the man in Galveston amplified. "Never knew her to turn down a prospective mother; keeps them until they are able to leave the hospital, and usually has a job waiting for them so they can keep their babies. He says if Angela Browning was burned up, to make mighty sure that there wasn't any funny stuff connected with it. The chief says she has officiated at more shotgun weddings than all the fathers of the moral South. He's pretty het up over it all."

"What do they say at the hospital?"

"You know hospitals; they won't tell anything. But the superintendent of nurses and another nurse left on the last interurban express for Houston. I think they are going up at Lomax's request to see if they can identify the body. Maybe you can beat that. There are several Houston women who have come down here for their babies to be born, just recently." He called off the names and addresses of half a dozen.

"That's good work, kid. Keep at it."

As Andy hung up the receiver, a copy boy dashed up to the desk with an armful of papers. Hunt glanced at the banner line and snatched up one.

WOMAN FIRE VICTIM IDENTIED

The *Record* had remade its first page, thirty minutes after its home edition was on the street. It disclosed that two Houston women had identified the body as that of Angela Browning, head of the Madonna Hospital in Galveston, and not that of her younger sister, Alice Blair.

It was a hurried makeover "fudge" of a hundred words, but it was a clean beat on the *Pioneer*. Hunt was beyond profanity.

The god who watches over cub reporters directed Sally Lomax to call her city editor just then. The story Sally had to tell turned him from a glowering tiger into a purring tomcat.

Sally had found Alice Blair.

5

At two o'clock, while Richard Lomax was berating the *Pioneer's* star reporter for purloining a postal money order from a dead man's pocketbook, the district attorney's sister Sally was sitting in her roadster, parked across South Main Boulevard from Alice Blair's deserted shop. The city editor had sent her out there to stand guard, presumably because "somebody ought to be out there" watching for the "unknown relatives" who might storm the doors. Then he had forgotten her.

Every one seemed to have forgotten her. She had had no lunch, no sleep; she wanted coffee. She had a headache. She wanted to know what was happening in the police station, in the district attorney's office, in the morgue, and most of all, in the *Pioneer* office. No one seemed to realize that this was her own special story; that if it hadn't been for her, the *Pioneer* would have been badly beaten. Here she was, after a perfectly swell piece of reporting, and they didn't even think enough of her to wonder if she wouldn't like to have some lunch. She had been sent out here to sit on the street and watch a door that no one was using, and wait until some one came out to take her place, if ever. It was a silly idea of old Andy Hunt's to have her out here, anyway. As if he wanted to get rid of her and that was the only way he could think of to do it.

Sally grew sorrier and sorrier for herself. Her headache flourished. Two blocks down the street there was a drugstore, where she could get coffee. She slid out from behind the wheel and walked wearily to the store. With a carton of hot coffee in one hand and two fat egg sandwiches in the other, she started back to her post. At the corner a blue roadster rounded the turn and all but ran her down before it stopped with a jerk. One look at the woman in the car, and Sally dropped the coffee.

Brown eyes frantic, face streaked with tears, lips white, it was Alice Blair leaning out of the car looking at her, not six feet away.

Sally was barely conscious of climbing into the car with the distraught girl; of driving with her into the rear court of the apartment house, going up the back stairs and into the apartment over the shop. When her mind had cleared, she was sitting on the side of Alice Blair's bed, trying to comfort the girl.

Neither of them had spoken since Sally had got into the car. Alice had pointed to three newspapers on the seat beside her—the noon and home editions of the *Pioneer,* and the first extra put out by the *Record.* Sally had glanced eagerly over the *Record's* front page as Alice drove into the court. When she had read rapidly the story that it was now thought to be Angela Browning dead in the morgue downtown, she was sure for the first time that she was not riding with the ghost of the girl she had identified early that morning by lantern light in a burned house.

And now, looking at the girl lying rigid beside her, Sally wondered what she could say, what she should say. *She* was guilty of that mistake!

"Angela!" Alice choked on the name.

"Do you think it may be your sister?"

The girl nodded. "The beaded bag, the underclothes— like mine." Little gasps. Sally had never before been in the presence of such grief. It wasn't noisy; just dry-eyed hysteria.

All at once Sally realized she had a great story; but she knew, too, that she must get this girl in hand before she could talk.

"Let me make you some strong coffee, Miss Blair," she suggested.

She went hastily back into the kitchen, through which they had entered the apartment. As she filled the coffee pot with water, put in the coffee, set out two cups and saucers, opened the ice box for cream, she planned her campaign. She found a dainty tray, put cups, cream and sugar on it, and went back to the bedroom.

"What can I do? What can I do?" Alice was sitting on the side of her bed. "I'm afraid, I'm afraid! Are they sure it is Angela?"

"I don't know, Miss Blair. We thought this morning it was you. Where were you?"

"In Galveston. I took a woman to the New York boat. I didn't see my sister. They said she had come to Houston last night. Where have they taken her?"

"Don't bother about that now, Miss Blair," soothingly. "You'd better lie down and get a little rest. You'll have to pull yourself together."

"I started back after the boat sailed at noon; I heard a boy yelling extra out in Harrisburg when I stopped for gas; I bought the papers. I don't know what to do. What must I do? How did Angela happen to be in that house?"

"Didn't you know this Martin Fox?"

"No! No! I never heard of him."

"Wait a minute! I smell that coffee boiling over." Sally dashed to the kitchen. When she came back, Alice had fallen back on the bed, hands clenched, staring at the ceiling.

"Here we are." Sally pushed back a book on the night table beside the bed, and set the tray on it. She pulled another pillow behind Alice's head. "There, that's good. Cream and sugar?"

There was a silence while they drank.

"Now, as soon as you are able, you ought to talk to my brother; he's the district attorney, you know. I'll phone him to come out here, and you tell him everything you know. Just let him handle all this hard part of it."

Alice nodded. It was a relief to let some one think for her.

Sally gulped the last of her coffee, and asked where she could find the telephone. Alice pointed to a door leading from the bedroom, and Sally went into the cheerful living-room, sophisticated, small, but in excellent taste. She closed the door behind her, and looked about for the telephone. It stood on a desk. Sally sat down, called the *Pioneer* office, asked for Andy Hunt.

"Listen, Andy!" Sally didn't realize that she had crashed into the inner circle with that salutation; she was too much intent on what she had to say. "Listen: I've got Alice Blair out here in her own apartment, and no one knows it." She sketched the story. The city editor, after his first credulous "Huh? Who?" said nothing but "Yes . . . Yes . . . Yes . . ." Sally knew his pencil was racing. Finally she had told him all she had to tell.

"Good enough, Sally. Now you stay there. Don't let any one know we have this. Phone me as soon as you get something else; as soon as your brother gets there and she tells her story to him. What about art?"

"I'll see. 'By." She held down the hook for a moment and called her brother's private office number. He answered at once.

"Dick?"

"Sally, I'm in a hurry. What is it?"

"Now you listen to me for a minute, Dick, and don't say one word while I'm talking. This is important. Hear me?"

"Yes, hurry up!"

"Alice Blair is in her apartment with me, and I want you to come out here as soon as you can."

"What?"

Patiently, Sally repeated the statement.

"Come alone, Dick, and don't let any one know where you are going. Will you?"

"I'll see."

"Dick Lomax! If you don't promise that, I'll take her away before you get here!"

"All right! All right! What's that address?"

By the time Dick arrived, Sally had Alice somewhat calmed. She had persuaded the girl to wash her face, and brush the dark red hair. A second cup of coffee had fortified each of them.

"Now, Miss Blair," Lomax began, when he was introduced, "I want you to tell me, as fully as possible, all you know about your sister's coming to Houston, where you have been, and what you know about Martin Fox. Take your time, but tell me everything. There's so much about this case that I don't understand."

"Do—do you—think she was—was murdered?"

"Do you, Miss Blair?"

"I—I don't know! I don't know!"

Skillfully Lomax got the girl started on the past history of the sisters; it would never do to let her get hysterical before he got that.

She told him how Angela had sent her to school in Virginia after their mother's death ten years back; then, recognizing her talent for design, had dispatched her to Paris for a year's study in the atelier of a great modiste; how, after she had returned, Angela had given her money to open the shop in Houston, where she had been more speedily successful than either she or Angela had anticipated. Little of this was news to the district attorney, but he let her tell the whole story in her own way.

"Now, Miss Blair, when did you see your sister last?"

"About ten days ago; I asked her up to dinner one evening, and she spent the night here with me, and went back to Galveston on an early interurban. I haven't seen her since then. I was told at the hospital yesterday evening that she had come up to Houston on business. She had left the hospital about seven o'clock last night, in an automobile, and they expected her back around midnight, they said."

"Had you ever heard her mention Martin Fox?"

"No, never. I remember that his family—or a family named Fox—lived in Longleaf, but I never saw him that I recall. I didn't even know he lived in Houston. I didn't know that my sister knew him."

"At what time did you leave Houston yesterday afternoon?"

"I left here just after the shop closed, about six o'clock, with Mrs. Caruthers, of New York, who had been visiting me. I drove her down in my own car. She was to sail for New York on the noon steamer to-day."

"And she did?"

"Yes. I saw her off on the boat and left at once for Houston."

She went on to tell how she and Mrs. Caruthers had met in Paris, where they had lived in the same pension. Mrs. Caruthers had been her agent both in Paris and New York since she had opened her shop in Houston. The New York buyer had come down to see her about the spring imports, had stayed here at her apartment while in Houston. They had had dinner the previous night at the Galvez Hotel, had spent the night there, had slept late that morning, breakfasted in their room, and had left the hotel to drive directly to the boat which sailed on time at noon. Alice had not stopped between the dock and Harrisburg, where she bought gasoline and the newspaper which gave her the first intimation of the tragedy. She had driven

blindly and without conscious purpose the six remaining
miles to her shop and home, stopping once to buy the later
papers. When a block from her shop, she had seen Miss
Lomax come out of the drugstore. Immediately she had
remembered Miss Lomax was a reporter, who would know
about the things the newspapers were printing. So she had
halted Sally.

That was her whole story, told in a voice that grew less
strained as she recited the commonplace facts. When she
had finished, she sat gazing sadly at Lomax, plainly waiting for his opinion. He was busily writing in his pocket
notebook. Finally she ventured, with an effort:

"Are you sure it is my sister?"

"Do you think you could stand seeing the body, Miss
Blair? It has been identified by two former maternity
patients of her hospital, and two nurses from there are
coming in on the next interurban; but I'd like you to see
it, too, to complete the identification."

"Oh, Dick, don't!" Sally implored. All during the interview she had been sitting silent, drinking hard onto key
words that she might write it all as Alice had told it. But
to take this distraught girl to see that disfigured body
Sally had seen earlier in the day seemed too brutal.

Alice had shrunk back in her chair and covered her eyes.

"Wait a minute," said Lomax. "It's four o'clock now;
those nurses must be here. I'll call my office and see." He
crossed to the telephone, and called his private number.
After a minute's talk with his secretary, he turned around.

"The superintendent of nurses and another nurse, a
Miss Stockard, have identified the body positively, Miss
Blair. They're at my office now. Shall I ask them to come
out here?"

She nodded, and he turned again to the telephone. When
he had finished, he told Alice, kindly, that he thought she
would better lie down until the two women arrived.

Fifteen minutes later, Sally admitted the nurses. Alice knew both slightly. They told her and the district attorney that Mrs. Browning had said the previous afternoon that she had to go to Houston on business, and at seven o'clock had driven off in a car with a man. Neither of them knew who the man was; Mrs. Browning had not mentioned his name. They had had no word of her until Mr. Lomax had summoned them to Houston. They had called at his office, and one of his assistants had taken them to the morgue. There was no doubt the body was that of Mrs. Browning. Alice shuddered and bit her lips as she heard the calm-voiced nurse say it. The woman was silent for a long minute. Then she turned to the district attorney.

"I must return to Galveston on the next interurban, Mr. Lomax," she said. "Some one must be in charge there to keep the hospital running. But I feel that Miss Stockard should stay here with Miss Blair. You ought to go to bed, Miss Blair," she added gently. Lomax nodded his approval.

He beckoned to the nurses to stay behind as Alice started into the bedroom.

"See that no one bothers her the rest of this afternoon and evening," he instructed. "She has a hard enough ordeal before her; this thing is only starting, you know, and she is going to be called on for a lot of trying work, I'm afraid. I don't think there is much she can do now, and she should rest before to-morrow. Don't let newspaper people get to her. If any one calls for her, try to find out who it is."

He and the superintendent left; Sally stayed long enough to ask for and get photographs of Alice and her sister, then dashed down the stairs and across the street to her roadster. She drove straight to the *Pioneer* office, taking the back streets for speed.

As she entered the city room, Andy Hunt got up and came to meet her. Sally was taking off her hat and coat.

"What's the rest of the story? Has any one else seen her? Did you get art?" Andy didn't wait, between questions, for answers.

"Pictures of Mrs. Browning and Miss Blair," Sally panted, handing the photographs to the city editor. "I have everything she told Dick. No one else knows she is there. I was there all the time she talked to him."

Andy turned and bawled down the city room to a loafing copy boy.

"Jim, tell the engraving room to rush two-column cuts of these. Fast!"

"Where did she find out about the death of her sister? God, girl, I've had a hard time, trying to keep from butting in out there and worrying for fear some one would find out she was there. If any one is in on this, I'll kill you. Now, where did she find out about her sister? Come over to my desk and sit in that chair." Andy sat down at his typewriter. As Sally talked, he wrote.

"All right: 'Alice Blair first learned of her sister's death by reading a *Pioneer* extra at Harrisburg at two o'clock this afternoon.' Go on from there; just the story as she told it to your brother."

He had written nearly two columns when she completed the story, taking a paragraph at a time out of his machine and thrusting it at the hovering copy boy. Ten minutes after he had pulled the last sheet out of his machine and rushed to the composing room with it, she heard the presses start. Sally's first private extra was about to hit the street.

She went over to the cooler and drank two cups of water, her hands trembling. Andy came back to the city room presently, half a dozen damp papers in his hand.

"Here you are, kid. It's a damn' fine story, and a clean beat. I'll raise you ten a week for this." Sally had never seen him so apparently pleased with the whole world.

Dumbly she took the paper from him. A fine story. A beat. A ten-dollar raise. She walked slowly to the far corner where stood her battered desk; sat down. She opened the paper and looked damply at the front page. There, under a banner headline, with a four-column spread of the pictures of the two sisters, she saw the magic, longed-for words over the story: *"By Sally Lomax."* Tears gushed into her eyes.

She read those three words over and over. Then she rose, hesitantly, and stumbled over to the city desk. Hunt, his feet propped up, was scanning down the story.

"Andy"—her voice was very small—"that's all right about the raise. Never mind it. Thank you for the by-line."

"Huh? Hell, kid, you had both coming to you! Have a cigarette? Now you trot along home and go to sleep. I want you down early in the morning."

Two hours later, while Sally was sleeping too soundly for such things to bother her, Richard Lomax was presiding over an interview between Alice Blair and a reporter from the *Bulletin*. For the third time that day he had been called down by an irate editor. Andy Hunt's generosity to Sally about the by-line had not been so magnanimous as it had seemed to her.

The *Bulletin's* rebuke was the most suave of the three. Its managing editor had simply asked him to explain how it was that the district attorney's sister happened to get an exclusive story from Alice Blair, when no other reporter even knew where she was.

Lomax, furious, had intimated that Hunt was the only editor in town who had had sense enough to keep a watch on the Blair apartment, but he had escorted the man from the *Bulletin* out to see Alice.

He left Miss Blair's resolved to compel Sally to quit the *Pioneer* at once.

He was coldly determined on the move as he dressed the next morning. When he went down to breakfast at eight o'clock, the cook, an old negress who had been Sally's nurse, informed him that Miss Sally had been gone nearly an hour.

"And she say her boss done raise her pay," Lulu added slyly. "I reckon we ought t' be right proud of Miss Sally."

The coffee scalded Dick's lips.

"Do you mind letting me read the paper?" he snarled at the amiable old servant.

She shuffled out. He was sure he heard her chuckle.

6

Thursday morning, when the mystery of the fire in which the beautiful nurse and the old collector had lost their lives was entering its second day, the *Morning-Bulletin* had its innings. Its city edition announced that the man who had driven with Angela Blair Browning from Galveston to Houston on the night before the fire had been identified. It named this man as Terence ("Terry") O'Toole, who three years before had served a six months' sentence in the Galveston County jail following a conviction of a violation of the federal prohibition laws. It delicately refrained from calling him a bootlegger.

In a signed story on the front page, Roscoe Eddy, the *Bulletin's* star man, told how he had stumbled upon a clew while driving to Galveston the previous night with Max Manning, chief investigator for the district attorney's office. They had talked to the night watchman on the drawbridge section of the Galveston causeway, which connects the mainland with Galveston Island.

The garrulous old man had divulged that he had seen "that red-headed woman that was burned up, in a car with Terry O'Toole, going to Houston."

"I know it was her," he said, "because the papers said the woman had on a gray fur coat and a little black hat. I didn't know her, but I knew Terry, and I spoke to him.

He just nodded to me when I yelled, 'Hi, there, Terry!'
and pulled his hat down over his eyes, like he was mad or
something."

O'Toole's car had been the first in a line of motors
halted at the drawbridge to allow an interurban train to
cross the narrow draw. It was half-past seven in the evening, then. That tallied with the time it would have taken
the car in which Mrs. Browning had left the hospital, as
reported by the nurses there, to reach the drawbridge.

The watchman thought "the woman with O'Toole must
have been mad, too, because her head was all sunk down in
the collar of her coat," and he had caught only a glimpse
of her red hair. The watchman had not seen O'Toole come
back from Houston to Galveston that night. It was entirely
possible that O'Toole had returned, because he lived in
Galveston, and unless there was a train demanding right
of way, cars did not stop at the drawbridge. Besides, the
watchman was not looking for O'Toole. If he hadn't read,
the next day, of the fire and the mystery growing out of it,
he would not have thought anything of seeing O'Toole and
the woman in the gray squirrel coat. Terry liked women
and women liked Terry, the watchman had heard tell.

No trace of O'Toole had been found in Galveston, although the police there, acting upon Manning's report,
had searched diligently.

O'Toole lived alone, Eddy's story recounted, in a cheap
cottage off the S Road, on the southwestern outskirts of
Galveston. He had been seen there last at noon on Wednesday, nearly ten hours after the fire had been discovered,
when a neighbor had noticed him drive away.

No one at the hospital could verify the fact that Mrs.
Browning knew O'Toole. The police thought it likely that
she did; her acquaintance among the underworld of the
coast city was extensive, because of the girls who took ref-
uge in her hospital.

The *Bulletin* also printed, in a box on its front page, a statement from the chief of the Galveston police, declaring again that he believed Mrs. Browning had gone to Houston on one of her errands of charity, connected with some girl who had gotten into trouble. The chief was open in his declaration that Mrs. Browning's death was probably not due to accident. He could not explain and would hazard no guess as to why she was in the house with the old man who was known to be a woman hater, even though he did come from the small town where she had been born.

The district attorney read this news after Lulu had told him Sally had already gone to work. It did little to soothe his feelings. Manning had no business letting Eddy print that stuff; he had no business taking a newspaper reporter along with him when he went to Galveston. Lomax went downtown with a dark brown taste in his mouth and a grudge against all reporters, his sister, Johnny Rorke, and Roscoe Eddy in particular.

The noon edition of the *Pioneer,* brought to him at ten-thirty that morning, didn't do much toward soothing him, either. It blazoned a story from Johnny Rorke, under a Galveston date-line, connecting Terry O'Toole with Alice Blair on the night of the fire.

Johnny had been routed from bed at six o'clock by Andy Hunt, who always read the *Bulletin* before he ate breakfast. Andy had ordered Rorke to take the first interurban for Galveston and to get more news on O'Toole than the *Bulletin* had. Johnny, by a lucky fluke, had found the night telephone operator of the Galvez Hotel at breakfast in the hotel coffee shop. She had, not without subsidy, been persuaded to talk.

She had told Johnny that on the night of February 14-15, a station-to-station call had come in from Houston to the hotel: a man had asked for Miss Alice Blair, registered there with a Mrs. Grace Caruthers. The girl had listened in on the conversation long enough to hear the man say, "Hell's broke loose now. She's found out about us." The girl had answered, "Yes, I know." Another call had interrupted the eavesdropping, and when the operator was able to open the key again, the girl had seemed to be angry or upset, and was telling the man, "For God's sake, don't do anything like that! Wait until I see you." To which the man in Houston had replied, "You poor kid, don't let it get you that way." Then the girl had said, "Well, I can't talk about it any more, now, Terry. Please, if you don't want to ruin us, don't do anything until I see her. Good-by."

The girl admitted that Miss Blair might have said Perry or Carey or Harry, but she thought it was Terry. She was sure she remembered the conversation correctly. The call had come in shortly before midnight; she was sure of that and the Houston office record would prove it, anyway.

As Lomax was digesting that story, his anger rising as he read, his secretary came in to say that Manning was calling from Galveston.

Manning told his chief it was advisable to get out a warrant for O'Toole's arrest, since he couldn't be found, high nor low, and if they had a warrant out, he could be brought in.

Lomax exploded.

"There's a lot of use getting a warrant out after you have let these newspapermen print the whole thing! O'Toole, like as not, is over in Louisiana by this time! What's got into you? Are you working for the state of Texas or for the newspapers?"

"Say, listen, Dick, these fellows help us more than they hinder us," Manning argued, aggrieved. "If Johnny Rorke hadn't known that dame at the Galvez, and I didn't ask him how he happened to hunt her up, do you think you'd know about that telephone call? Did Miss Blair tell you about it? Huh!"

"Well, they'd better be careful printing that sort of thing. Suppose O'Toole can explain all of this? I hope he slaps a libel suit on them." Nothing would appease Lomax to-day.

"Fat chance for a libel suit from a fellow who has been in jail for bootlegging! What does the Blair girl have to say about all this?"

"I'm after her now," Lomax said. "Call me back in two hours."

Dick hung up the receiver, phoned an assistant to go downstairs and swear out a warrant for O'Toole's arrest, and put on his hat. He would go out and see the Blair girl himself. He had been putting off calling her since he had got to the office, because there was a mass of work facing him, and he wanted a clear hour ahead when he went after her. Just as he started out the door, he turned. Maybe he had better call her up first; he didn't want to wait while she dressed or puttered around. There was no answer! For a minute, Lomax's heart almost failed him. Could the girl have escaped during the night? Could O'Toole have come in and gone off with her?

Still a little fearful, although his common sense told him the girl certainly would have done nothing like that, he hurried down to his car, parked in the rear driveway, and sped out Main Boulevard faster than even he had any right to go. He parked near the Blair shop, recognizing Sally's yellow roadster standing in the side street. What on earth could she be doing out here? He would give that young woman a piece of his mind.

He went up the steps three at a time, without ringing, and knocked on the living-room door. Sally opened it.

"Dick! I don't think you'd better come in. Miss Stockard and I can't do a thing with her! She's simply collapsed!"

"What are you doing here?" He walked past her. In the bedroom beyond he could hear hysterical moans and the soothing voice of the nurse.

"She insisted on going down to see the body," Sally whispered. "She's been like this ever since we got back. We can't stop her."

"Well, what are you doing here? I gave Miss Stockard orders last night that no one was to see Miss Blair unless I gave permission."

"Darling! Miss Stockard knew I was your sister, and she didn't bother about me!"

"Sally, I've had all of this I'll stand! You'll have to stop this newspaper nonsense at once. I won't have it! You're embarrassing me beyond endurance with the other papers! You've got to quit! You hear me?"

"Tut! Tut! What will you do, Dick dear? Put me out in the street? Disown me? I'll make my living, just the same. Andy Hunt gave me a ten-dollar raise for that signed story yesterday."

Sally had closed the door into the bedroom; she was enjoying thoroughly the tiff with her brother.

"I'm making thirty-five a week now. You ought to be proud of me!"

Before Dick could frame a reply, Miss Stockard came in.

"Good morning, Mr. Lomax. I think Miss Blair will be quite all right now. I've given her a triple bromide. She's dropping off to sleep right now, and I think she'll stay asleep most of the day. She didn't sleep an hour all last night."

"You've done what?"

"Given her a sedative; she had to get some rest." Belle Stockard was as impersonal and dictatorial as young nurses grow; she had never come into contact with a district attorney before, but she was not impressed. Her first duty was to her patient.

"My Lord, woman, I've got to talk to that girl!"

"Not now, Mr. Lomax. She won't be able to tell you anything until she wakes and that won't be for several hours, at least." Miss Stockard vanished on noiseless feet into the bedroom.

"Well, I'm going," said Sally nonchalantly. Her brother, after glaring at the closed door, regretting that he was a gentleman, went over to it and knocked. Miss Stockard came out, plainly annoyed.

"You should not have put Miss Blair under a drug until I had been consulted," he said sternly. "It was highly necessary that I discuss some of the details of this case with her. I'm sure you didn't realize that," he added hastily, as the nurse stiffly asked in the same breath:

"Is Miss Blair a prisoner simply because her sister happens to have been killed, Mr. Lomax?"

"No! No! Certainly not! But I need information that only she can give me." He softened diplomatically. "You are sure she will sleep most of the day?"

"Certainly!" If Miss Stockard was not sure, she wouldn't admit it to this person.

"Very well; just see that *no one* is admitted without orders from me, and telephone me as soon as she wakes. Meanwhile, I'd muffle the telephone bell. Don't answer any questions put to you by newspapermen, and don't discuss what you may find out about the case with any one, please. I don't wish to be disagreeable, Miss Stockard; I am merely carrying out my duties as district attorney in giving you such instructions."

Sally, who had been listening on the landing, preceded him down the stairs. Each drove off after a cool "See you later" from Sally and a stiff touch of the hat from her brother.

Sally parked her roadster around the corner from the *Pioneer* office and went in to report.

The case was at a standstill the rest of the day, the afternoon editions merely adding to the Galveston telephone operator's disclosures the fact that a warrant had been sworn out for the arrest of Terence O'Toole, "a convicted bootlegger and said to be a friend of both the Blair sisters," as a material witness. As yet, there had been no report made public on the autopsy over the two bodies. O'Toole apparently had vanished off the edge of the earth in his car, although the police and county authorities of the two cities and counties predicted his early apprehension. Late in the afternoon, Lomax offered two-hundred-and-fifty-dollars' reward for information leading to O'Toole's arrest, and the chief of police in Galveston announced that city would give a like amount.

The collapse of Alice Blair after viewing her sister's body was told in a story in the *Pioneer* written by Sally, and imparted hastily by Lomax to the other papers. The district attorney added to his statement that she was in seclusion under the care of a nurse from her sister's hospital, and that no one was allowed to see her "under orders from her physician." That no physician had been called in was a minor matter to Lomax; he had to appear to be shielding the prostrated girl.

Johnny Rorke was off on a secret errand of his own; he had returned from Galveston early in the afternoon and asked for the afternoon off; Andy, used to his star reporter's more or less mysterious methods of getting news, readily consented.

"You'd better wait around the office," Andy told Sally. "Something may turn up."

Something did turn up. At a quarter to five, Belle Stockard telephoned to Sally.

"This is my regular night off, and I've got to go back to Galveston," the nurse said. "Could you come out and spend the night with Miss Blair? She's all right, but I don't want to leave her alone, you know. All she needed was sleep, and I think she'll sleep the clock around. I talked with the superintendent in Galveston and she thinks it

will be all right, if you can come out. I'll be back early in
the morning, and we won't say anything about my being
away."

Sally would be pleased to be of any assistance to Miss
Stockard and Miss Blair. She would be right out. No, she
hadn't had supper. All right, she would eat before she
came. Would Miss Stockard call her brother and assure
him that Miss Blair would sleep all night, and then no one
would be bothered? Miss Stockard would be glad to do so.

"You carry a rabbit's foot, kid," chuckled Andy, when
Sally told him of the arrangement, after swearing him to
secrecy.

"Oh, I reckon this nurse has just got a heavy date in
Galveston, and then Dick made her mad this morning,"
Sally said. "If I get anything to-night, I'll take care to
write it so this Stockard girl won't get in bad."

"That's the stuff; never betray a news source," Andy
approved. He solemnly shook hands with her. "If you can
contrive to make a little racket and wake up the Blair girl
and get her to talking . . . well, let your conscience be
your guide and remember that a reporter needs a collapsible
conscience. If she will spill anything about O'Toole . . .
um . . . good luck, kid!"

When Sally arrived, the nurse was ready to leave. Alice
was still sleeping soundly.

Once the nurse had gone, Sally prowled around the
apartment. Suddenly she remembered that she must telephone Lulu that she wouldn't be home that night; she decided to say that she was going to Galveston on an assign-
ment from the paper. She closed the door between the
bedroom and the living-room and called her home. She
lied like an old hand at it, blushing a bit at the old housekeeper's admonition to take good care of herself and not
drive too fast, and not to go "messin' around Galveston
without a good man or a *po*-lice along with you."

The desk upon which the telephone stood, like everything else in the small apartment, reflected its owner's good taste and sophisticated daintiness, but on it was a gaudy, heart-shaped candy box of five-pound size, much too ornate. Sally had noticed it before when she had sat there to telephone; now it irritated her even more. She took off the lid. On the half-eaten top layer of candies was a lace-paper valentine. She idly opened that to the second page, on which was written in a large, clumsy hand: "To the Little Copperhead from her Big Rattler."

She replaced the valentine guiltily, and closed the box. Under the edge of it now was showing a corn-colored envelope. She pulled that out. It was addressed to Miss Alice Blair, at the apartment, in a woman's neat, vertical handwriting. It was postmarked at Galveston, Feb. 14, 6:30 a.m. That was Tuesday, Sally counted back, the day before the fire on Wednesday morning.

Sally debated. Should she be a lady and replace the letter, or a reporter and read it? She put it down, undecided, and looked around for her purse to get a cigarette. It held none; she had left the packet on her desk at the office. She wandered about the living-room, looking for Alice Blair's supply, tiptoed into the bedroom, opening the door carefully and closing it behind her. In the semi-darkness of the curtained room she stumbled into a chair, barking a shin, creating an incredible noise. The girl in the bed sat up.

"Who's that?" she whispered hoarsely.

Sally's heart was in her mouth. She was a little frightened, sympathetically, sensing the fear in the other girl's voice.

"It's—it's just me—Sally Lomax," she said softly. "I'm so sorry I woke you." She went to the bed and put an arm about Alice Blair's shoulders. "Try to go back to sleep. I'm just staying here with you while Miss Stockard is away for a little while, and I stumbled over a chair."

"Miss Stockard?" Alice was not fully awake.

"The nurse who is staying with you," Sally supplied. "But you go back to sleep, honey."

The girl's hands went up to cover her face. Sally, expecting more hysterics, patted her shoulder, reassuringly. Suddenly Alice's hands came down, her head up.

"How long have I been asleep?"

"Since before noon."

"What time is it now?"

Sally glanced at her wrist in the half light.

"A quarter after six. You'd better try to get some more sleep, honey." This was half honest, half hypocritical, Sally knew, but she did want to do the right thing.

"I'm all upset inside. I think I'll fix a cup of tea. My mouth is terribly dry."

"I'll make it," said Sally eagerly. "You just lie down; wait a minute. I'll bring you a glass of water." She pushed Alice gently back onto the pillow.

But while Sally was reaching for the tea canister, with the water on to boil, Alice appeared in the kitchen doorway, a lavender quilted robe over her nightgown, lavender satin mules on her absurdly tiny feet.

"My head is so fuzzy," she complained, rubbing one slender, long-fingered hand across her forehead, "I think I'd rather have coffee than tea. Do you mind?"

The reporter and the good Samaritan struggled again within Sally. The reporter won. "Coffee it shall be," she agreed, grinning.

They drank it, black and strong, in the living-room, and ate bread and butter sandwiches which Sally had made while the coffee brewed and Alice took a bath.

After her second cup, Alice, wandering about nervously, paused at the desk and picked up the big candy box. She opened it, put its lid down on the desk, laid the gaudy valentine in it, and came over to Sally with the box.

"Have some candy?"

Sally took a piece, as casually as she could. She was glad she didn't have to face that valentine. Alice took out a piece, then replaced the sentimental lace paper atrocity and the lid. As she did so, she noticed the corn-colored envelope beside the box. A bit too quickly for the action to appear as casual as she evidently wished her guest to consider it, if Sally happened to be looking, she stuffed it into a pigeonhole of the desk. Sally had missed nothing of this.

She was curled up in a low modernistic chair. Alice went over to the *chaise longue* and stretched out.

It was a strange situation, the reporter reflected as she lighted a cigarette. They might be any two girls in college, with their cigarettes and a box of candy, ready for a long gossip on the sins of the faculty, the coming prom, the newest beau, and what they would do when they had been graduated. She had to force herself to realize that they were in the shadow of a great tragedy, each waiting for the other to start a discussion of how it had happened, why it had happened, and what might come of it. Sally was embarrassed; she didn't know what to say first. Alice spared her the trouble.

"Will you tell me just what has happened since I went to sleep this morning?" she asked. "What have they found out?"

"Mighty little. Really almost all we know is that your sister came to Houston the other night in a car with a man named Terry O'Toole, and that no trace of him can be found now, although they have offered a five-hundred-dollar reward. What's the matter?"

Alice was bolt upright, her face stricken with a new terror.

"Terry doesn't know anything about it! Terry didn't have anything to do with it!" The words tumbled out.

"Was it he who telephoned you before midnight at the Galvez—that night?" Sally asked, as easily as she could manage to say it.

"How did you know that?" Alice was almost in a panic now.

"A telephone girl listened in. But don't be alarmed. Why don't you tell me all about Terry? There's no reason to be afraid of my knowing; maybe you'll feel better if you talk it all out." Sally felt like a sneak—but maybe it would help the girl. She had heard it helped people to talk their troubles out at a time like this.

Alice pondered, biting her lips. Suddenly she turned to look Sally in the eyes.

"Maybe you're right! I'll tell you."

She gulped the last of the coffee, and settled back a little more easily.

"Terry and I are in love with each other; we have been for some time. But I've been afraid to tell Sister; she always has objected to my having any men friends—any friends at all who might be called intimate, even girls. She was an awful prude about men; just as soon as I got interested in some boy or he got interested in me, Sister scared him off. . . . But Terry doesn't know anything about—about this horrible thing that happened to her. I *know* he doesn't!"

"Did you know that he drove your sister up to Houston in his car Tuesday night?"

"Of course I did! That's why he telephoned me at the Galvez. He was coming up here, and she said she had an engagement here, and wanted to talk to him anyway, and so they came up together in his car. He told her on the way up that we were in love with each other and he meant to give up his—his business—that he was in, and marry me and go to California to live. She got white hot and went at him like a snake, he said. He called me up at the hotel to ask me what to do about it and to warn me she was on the warpath. I told him not to do anything until I could see him, and then he said the best thing for us to do was for him to close out his—business, and for us to get married right away, and go away until she cooled off. He said he would go back and tell Angela—wherever she was—he didn't say—and tell her we were going to do that. I told him for God's sake not to do any such thing. But he laughed and said he liked to hear her rave. I told him to see me first—be sure to wait until he saw me.”

Sally felt a little thrill run up her spine; that was just what the telephone girl had overheard them say. This was a true story!

“Terry didn't know anything about handling Sister when she got angry,” Alice was going on. “I have always been a little afraid of her when she got very mad; I have sometimes felt she might do something dangerous. I wonder—do you suppose she could have gotten angry at some one who set fire to that house to kill her while she was in one of her rages? I'm going mad with this! If I only knew what happened after Terry left her—wherever he left her!”

The girl's hands were shaking. Sally knew she must get her off that line of thought, or Alice would be just as she had been after she had seen her sister's body.

“Your sister was a good deal older than you, wasn't she?”

“Nearly eight years older. She was the most wonderful sister and friend in the world, except for her funny attitude about my men friends. When our mother died, I was about fourteen. She came to Longleaf and sold the house we lived in and took me off with her. First she put me in a convent in San Antonio, and then the next year in a college in Virginia. When I graduated there, she sent me to Paris for more than a year, and when I came home she gave me enough money to start my shop.” Alice was repeating facts she had already told, but Sally did not remind her of that.

"Did you see her often after you came here?" she prompted.

"No, I didn't. She seemed to want to keep our relationship as quiet as she could. She had come to Galveston as a nurse just before Mother's death. She started her hospital down there partly on the money from the sale of our old home, and she always told me that my education was only her payment of my share. I didn't care; she was older and I always felt she had a much better business head than I had. Then after I came back from Paris, she already had the plan for this shop, and I was awfully busy getting it on its feet. We didn't see each other oftener than once a month. Was that odd? I never thought of it that way. You see, we had never been much together. I had been away to school, and before Mother's death she had been away from home since I was just a little girl. Sister was more like a very, very dear friend, but one of the kind you don't see much of."

"Do you know anything about her husband? Is he dead?"

"I think so. Before Mother died, we knew she had married. She wrote us that she had, and a little later, she wrote that she had left her husband. She only said his name was Browning; I don't believe I ever heard her mention his first name. When I left Longleaf with her, she said she didn't want to talk about her marriage; she made that statement casually one day, as though she was afraid I might ask questions about him. So I never pried into it.

"I don't know a great deal about Sister's life after she went off to study nursing. I didn't even know that she had started a maternity hospital or why, except what she wrote me, that first year I was in Virginia in school, about it. She said, 'You know my keen interest in mothers and children.' I thought that was funny, because I didn't really know what her interests were, except in me."

Alice lighted a cigarette. Her hands were steadier now, and her voice had almost lost its tremble.

"After I came here and started the shop, I learned that her chief interest actually was in what she called 'unfortunate girls.' She usually had two or three unmarried girls in the hospital. I met some of them. The nurses have told me all those girls thought Sister was a saint. Well, I suppose she was." Alice sighed. "A curious mixture of saint and devil. In some ways she was the red-headedest woman I ever knew."

"How did you happen to meet Mr. O'Toole? Through your sister?" Sally was carefully casual.

"Yes. They had known each other several years, and Sister and I met him on the beach one day and she introduced him to me." For the first time Alice seemed to be keeping something back; her tones were not as easy as they had been. Then her eyes grew black in their intensity.

"It's perfectly senseless for any one to suspect Terry of doing this thing—or even being mixed up with it. In the first place, I'm sure he wasn't even in Houston when the—the fire happened. I'm sure he came back to Galveston just after he talked to me over the telephone."

"Why are you sure of that?"

"Well—he said he was starting back right then. And I know he told me the truth. Terry always tells me the truth. Besides, he wasn't angry at Sister; he was just amused. I tell you, he didn't realize the danger in her rages. It just made him laugh!"

The girls sat silent. What Alice was thinking she kept to herself. Sally was deep in new theories of the crime. Could Terry have been an old lover of Angela's? Was Angela really a man-hater? How did she and old Fox, a man without a woman in his life, happen to be out there together? Perhaps, after all, this was just an accident, as they had at first thought it was. Ordinary things could happen, perfectly casual, commonplace things, in such strange sequences that, when you put three or four of them together, they made a sinister thirteen.

Well, it would be a tragic joke if this should turn out to be nothing but an accident. Suppose Angela Blair had gone up to Houston, on some harmless mission, had met old Martin Fox, and they had sat down over a bottle of whiskey to talk about the old home town. They had got drunk and he turned the lamp over. But— Sally sat up with a start. She must be getting woozy; what about all that kerosene-soaked newspaper in the stair closet, all that kerosene spread over the carpet and up on the bed? No! No!

"No, what?" Alice had jumped at Sally's exclamation.

"No. No, I didn't mean anything. I was just thinking so hard I talked aloud. My dear! Don't you want to go to bed? I've been thoughtless. You must be tired!"

"I'm not in the least sleepy. Remember, I slept all day." Alice smiled sympathetically. "Are you tired?" Sally shook her head.

"Well, then, if you are sure." She paused, pondered, went on: "Miss Lomax, have you heard anything more about those whiskey glasses they found in that house?"

"No, I haven't." Sally hesitated, remembering how Miss Blair's assistants had snubbed her for such a question. "Did your sister drink—I mean, could she have been drinking too much out there?"

"I don't know." Alice's face was troubled. "I know she hated Prohibition; I've heard her say it was worse than the open saloons had ever been. I've seen her take a drink now and then, as most people do, nowadays. But I never heard of or saw her taking too much. You see, my sister was such a careful person in other ways, I can't imagine her drinking enough liquor to make her stupid. That's the thought that comes back to me all the time. Because of that I can't believe it was an accident."

"If it was foul play, what do you think could have been the motive?"

"If I only knew! If it was murder—but it couldn't have been! Who would want to kill her? She was such a useful person; so kind!"

"Do you have any idea where that husband of hers could be?"

Alice looked up suddenly.

"Why—do you mean he might have murdered her? Oh, he's dead. At least she always spoke of him as though he were dead—the few times I ever heard her mention him. I'm sure he is."

"Well, of course, that was just an idea of mine. Another thing I'd like to ask you, and I hope you won't think I'm impertinent: where do you suppose Mr. O'Toole is? Why doesn't he get in touch with you?" Sally made the question in her most ordinary tone, but the response was not as matter of fact as Sally's voice had been.

"If I only knew! If I could only see and talk to Terry! Why doesn't he call me? Why doesn't he come here?" She broke into racking sobs.

Sally knelt by the *chaise longue* and put her arms about the weeping girl.

"There, there," she soothed. "He has a good reason for not coming. You know that, don't you?"

Alice nodded and clung tighter.

"It's so terrible! So terrible! And I'm so afraid! I don't know what to do! I must do something! I must do something!"

The storm subsided. Sally got a cigarette for Alice and held a light for her, lighted one for herself, and, pulling her chair closer, sat down and patted Alice's hand.

"I suppose they will let me bury my sister up home, won't they?" Alice spoke timidly, as though she feared the law might keep her sister's body from her. The question wrung Sally's heart more than anything that had happened in all the evening.

"Of course. That can all be attended to for you, Miss Blair. Why don't you talk to my brother about it—or would you rather I'd ask him in the morning?"

"I'll do it. I'll have to do all those things tomorrow. I'll go down to the bank in the morning and ask them to look after the hospital; Sister always told me to go to my bank and have them see about such things, if anything happened to her. The bank has her will, I know. I don't know what to do about that hospital—I can sell a woman a dress, but I wouldn't know how to go about running a maternity business." Alice smiled ruefully.

This was a good beginning, and Sally seized upon it. She started a discussion of clothes, of the Paris conception of dressmaking as a fine art, of the distinctive manners of each great Parisian *couturière*. Alice met her effort gallantly. They talked until Alice's eyes drooped wearily. Sally made her go to bed; it was long after midnight. Sally spread a blanket for herself on the *chaise longue,* as Miss Stockard had done the night before. More exhausted than she had realized, presently she was sound asleep.

7

Together the two girls cooked breakfast and sat in the sunny breakfast nook off the kitchen to eat it. Alice's eyes were brighter and her manner more determined; she was saner, somehow, this morning. It was past nine o'clock when they rose from the table. Neither had mentioned the overhanging tragedy while they had cooked and eaten; there was a gentle consideration evident in each for the other.

As she started toward the bedroom, Alice turned to her guest.

"I'm so grateful to you for staying here with me last night and for letting me talk myself weary," she said. "I feel this morning that I can start all my work with my nerves calmer, at least, than they were yesterday. It has been nice to have some one here who was understanding, not just sympathetic."

"Why—" Sally was at a loss to cope with this calm woman.

"I'll telephone Miss Stockard in Galveston," Alice was going on, with just a pat on Sally's arm to stop whatever she might start to say, "that she needn't bother to come back to-day."

Sally nodded. "Before you put in that call, I'll phone my office and see if there is anything new," she said, "if you don't mind."

Johnny Rorke answered when she asked for the city desk. He greeted her gayly, congratulated her on the "lucky breaks" she had been getting.

"Stop it, Johnny," she said. "Is there anything new on the story to-day?"

Morphine had been found in the stomachs of both Mrs. Browning and old Fox, he told her. The chemist also had found traces of morphine sulphate in the whiskey glasses which had stood on the bare pine table in the kitchen of the old house on Telephone Road.

Johnny stopped in the midst of his story to tell Sally to watch Alice closely when she repeated it to her. Alice, turning from the window where she had been standing, had caught the look on her guest's face. She had come close beside the desk to whisper, "Tell me! Tell me! What is it?" Sally reached out a hand and gently pushed her away, nodding to her while she listened to Rorke.

"Do you get it, Sally?" he was saying, slowly and earnestly. "This means that whoever planned the burning of the house did not mean for either of those two people to leave it alive! It means, beyond any doubt, that not only was it premeditated murder of the woman, but also of the man. No chance of an accident here, now."

"Anything else new?"

"You mean have they found O'Toole? No. Where that bird slipped to, I'd like to know. He's got the answer to this thing in his pocket. Does she know where he might be—I mean, has she said anything that would indicate that she might know where he is hiding?"

"Nothing. And I don't think so."

Sally hung up the receiver and turned to Alice. She hated to tell the girl this last thing; but some one had to do it.

"Your sister was—there was morphine in her stomach." She spoke gently. But Alice did not faint, nor even flinch.

She stood staring at Sally; the girl could almost see her thoughts taking form.

"It was murder—sure, sure murder." There was a new note in the low voice, a vindictive note. Suddenly the thought came to Sally: Alice Blair would feel that she must avenge her sister's murder—the sister who had done everything for her—had been "the best friend a girl ever had; the most generous friend."

"Whoever killed her wanted to be sure. Drugged with morphine and left to burn!"

The voice was still calm, but the great brown eyes were no longer brown, nor yet black with enlarged pupils. Sally felt a tremor of fear; the woman standing before her had *red* eyes! She had seen Siamese cats glare with that same queer radiance.

Alice sat down in one of the big, deep chairs. She looked out the window again at the line of cars going up and down Main Boulevard, men hurrying late to their offices, housewives going to market, mothers taking children to school. Sally was silent. There seemed to be nothing she could say.

Alice got up, briskly.

"It was extraordinarily kind of you to take pity on me last night, Miss Lomax." She spoke as though she had not already thanked Sally for staying. "Whatever happens to me in the rest of my life, I'll always be grateful to you for that. You have no idea how much it meant to me. Now I mustn't keep you from your office longer. I will phone you, please believe me, when I have anything to tell a newspaper. That much I can do to repay you."

Sally stood up uncertainly; she was being dismissed. Alice went on:

"I am going down to the bank now, and then I think I'll go over to see your brother. I must telephone down to the hospital at Galveston. I must see about funeral arrangements for my sister. I must find out what happened to that maid of mine. I must get in touch with the girls in the shop downstairs."

"I hope you will call me if there is a single thing I can do for you," Sally said, warmly. "I mean beyond anything I can do as a reporter. And if you find anything that my paper can help you with, please let us know. If I am not there, ask for Mr. Hunt or Mr. Rorke."

"I will, Miss Lomax—do you mind if I call you Sally?"

"Oh, please do! I've been on the verge of saying Alice half a dozen times."

They kissed as two old friends when Sally had put on her hat. She went down the back stairs to her car and drove slowly to the *Pioneer* office. When she appeared in the city room, Hunt and Rorke, warmly cordial, proposed to go down to the corner restaurant. Most of the big stories were plotted down there; it was the only place Hunt could be free from the enslaving telephone, ravenous printers, and visiting pests. The noon edition was out, and Andy demanded his mid-morning coffee.

"This morphine in old man Fox's stomach is sure a rum go," said Rorke when the greasy Greek waiter had brought the three thick cups of fine coffee and had gone back to the front window to gaze mournfully out at the street. "I had this thing all doped out—"

"For crying out loud!" Hunt growled. "Your puns are in miserable taste! Morphine—rum go—all doped out! Criminy! We all had it fixed up that way, bright boy: old man gets the woman completely blotto and pours kerosene around, turns over the lamp, and is so drunk himself that he burns up before he can get out of the house. He's all aflame with burning oil; he tries to open the front door he had locked. In his frenzy, he breaks off the key when it won't work in the old lock. Lord, boy, I've had that figured out since the first morning. Why he wanted to burn her up was the one thing I couldn't explain. Sally, what do you think about the O'Toole end of the thing—that is, what do you think Alice Blair thinks about him?"

Sally repeated, as briefly as she could, what Alice had told her about Terry, about the telephone conversation at the Galvez, and Alice's apparent sincerity in declaring that O'Toole had nothing to do with the crime in the old house. "Somehow she made me believe that he didn't, too," she concluded.

"Well, kid, you may believe it, but it don't look so good for the romantic Terry, just the same," Johnny commented dryly. "Her own story damns him still more completely. He has been a bootlegger; everybody knows that. May be one yet. The old man and the woman had been drinking whiskey. What was to keep Terry from going out there after he telephoned Alice, getting drunk along with them, telling Angela that he and Alice were going to be married anyway, and having her unleash her celebrated wildcat rage on him, and then knock them both off: Angela because she had threatened him, maybe, with something she had on him, then the old man because he was a witness? You can't tell what Angela Browning had on O'Toole. She knew her underworld, baby. And drunk men have done such things as kill women."

"Oh, you're crazy," said Sally sharply. "You can't believe anything as improbable as that."

Andy cut in grumpily.

"I'd like to know what time O'Toole got back to Galveston from Houston—how long he slept in that house of his out on the S Road before that neighbor saw him drive off at noon. Yes, sir, I'd like to know that one thing." He pushed back his chair, and rose. "Well, folks, I've got to get back upstairs. Johnny, you'd better see what Lomax has to say this morning."

"Want to go over and see the big brother, Sally?"

"No, thank you, Johnny. I'm keeping out of his way as much as possible. I'm not the fair-haired sister since that story the other night."

Andy grinned at her, almost affectionately.

"That's all right. You come along upstairs with me. I'd like to keep you handy; if something breaks to-day maybe you'll be able to use some of this 'confidential dope' you got out there last night."

Johnny sat around the district attorney's office for the next hour, talking to Monroe and Eddy, who were marking time there, too. They saw Alice Blair go in for a conference with Lomax, they saw her leave. She was polite to them, but she had "nothing to say." Lomax would tell them only that Miss Blair had come in to talk about funeral arrangements for her sister's body; at his suggestion she had postponed doing anything about it for another twenty-four hours.

"What do you expect to break in twenty-four hours, Dick? Arrest O'Toole?"

"No predictions, Roscoe. I'd like to arrest him right now, if you care for that information!" Lomax smiled ruefully.

It was one o'clock when he appeared again in the outer office, where the three reporters were playing penny ante.

"I've got an important statement for you fellows," he said. "Arthur has made carbon copies of it for each of you. The only reason I'm giving it to you is because the reporters in Key West got hold of this woman, and you'll be deviling me anyway, and I might as well give it to you straight. This was dictated to my stenographer over long distance from Key West."

"Who the hell is in Key West, Lomax?"

"Well, I expected you bright boys would have forgotten that! Mrs. Grace Caruthers, who was Alice Blair's guest here and in Galveston, is in Key West!"

Rorke and Monroe grabbed the sheets of paper Lomax handed them and made for telephones. Home edition deadlines were near for both afternoon papers.

The Florida authorities, at the request of District Attorney Lomax, had boarded the Galveston-New York steamer that Friday morning when it had touched Key West and had questioned Mrs. Caruthers. The dress importer had freely admitted that she had spent the night of the double murder with Alice Blair, and that prior to that time, she had been Miss Blair's guest in Houston for two days. And Mrs. Caruthers had innocently disclosed that Miss Blair had been away from their room in the hotel from about midnight until six o'clock in the morning!

"Miss Blair received a telephone call over long distance about eleven-thirty o'clock on Tuesday night. [Mrs. Caruthers's statement was quoted.] "Apparently she was much distressed over the news she received. She cried for a little while, and then asked me if I didn't want to go for a drive along the beach. I did not go, because I sleep badly on shipboard, and wanted a good night's rest. Miss Blair said she was not afraid to go alone; that she frequently drove alone at night, and that she could just drive up and down the beach until she was sleepy. She had parked her car in the driveway in front of the hotel.

"I dropped off to sleep a little after twelve [the statement continued] and was awakened when Miss Blair returned to the room. She was exhausted and haggard. My watch showed a quarter of six. I did not ask her where she had been during the six hours she had been gone. She fell asleep almost at once, and slept for about four hours. She awakened me by calling out in her sleep; I don't know what she said. But I arose and began packing my things. I awakened her at ten o'clock.

"We had breakfast in our room and she drove me over to the steamer. On the way Miss Blair apologized for the disturbance of the night before, saying that her sister had discovered that she was in love with a man and that he had telephoned her that her sister was very angry about it. She told me: 'My sister is jealous of every man who looks at me twice; I've never had anything on my conscience except in deceiving her. I hate quarrels and scenes, and this one upset me terribly.'

"After the boat had sailed I saw a Houston newspaper extra that some one had brought aboard, and saw that the headline said something about the discovery of two bodies in a fire. I did not read the paper; naturally I did not connect the fire and tragedy with my friend. I had my usual attack of seasickness that evening, and did not leave my cabin until the boat touched here at Key West and you gentlemen asked for me.

"I have known Alice Blair for more than three years; I met her in Paris and I consider her a fine young woman. She has a real success ahead of her in her business."

A messenger dashed off with the copy for Andy Hunt while Johnny was telling him enough of it for the city editor to be able to write the headlines while the boy was getting from the courthouse to the *Pioneer* office. No one bothered to tell Sally the cause of the mild commotion at the city desk. She read of it first in the home edition, and had just completed her astonished perusal when Johnny sauntered into the city room. Sally hurried after him to the city desk. He turned and surveyed her pityingly.

"Well, kid, this looks awkward for your little girl friend," he taunted.

"What do you mean?"

"Well, if your brother doesn't arrest her as a suspect in this murder, I'll buy you a coky-coly." Johnny pushed his hat far back on his head and balanced himself on feet spread wide apart.

"Arrest Alice? Tommyrot! How could he?"

"How couldn't he, now?"

Sally turned to Andy as the oracle to vindicate her. But Andy was whittling on a match, a habit of his when he was dovetailing the corners of a troublesome story. She whirled back to Johnny, more loquacious than Andy, always.

"Listen, Sally: Alice Blair was away from the Galvez for six hours. She could drive to Houston at that time of the night in two hours, help O'Toole get the woman and the old man drunk, put the poison pills in their whiskey, soak the house in kerosene, start the fire and get back to Galveston in another two hours, having had one hundred and twenty minutes to complete the job in the old house." Johnny's voice was matter-of-fact. "What's more, all she has to say about this story is, 'I have nothing to say!' I called her, George called her, Roscoe called her."

"That's just nonsense! Alice Blair didn't have one thing to do with that affair, and I believe every word when she says Terry O'Toole didn't! You can't honestly believe such a wild story, Johnny!"

"No? And just when I was beginning to have hopes of you, too!" The star reporter's voice was maliciously mocking. "Well, she may 'have nothing to say,' but I'll bet Alice wishes that her talkative friend in Key West had kept her mouth half as well closed as Alice has. The old gal sure spilled a mouthful."

Sally wanted to cry. She hated newspapermen when they got so cynical and sour on the world! She was almost sorry that she was going to be a newspaperman herself, all the rest of her life, please God.

"You're wanted over there on the telephone, Sally." Andy Hunt had heard the office boy call her, although Sally hadn't. She picked up the phone on Andy's desk; the girl was so furious that she forgot this was the city editor's sacred line.

"Put that call for me here," she snapped. There was a click on the wire and her brother's voice came over it. "Oh, hello, Dick! What do you want?"

Andy Hunt dropped his match and looked up.

"Sally, do you think you could spend the night with Alice Blair to-night?" Dick Lomax was blandly asking.

"Spend the night with her? Why?"

"I don't want to arrest her to-night for a certain reason, if I can get out of it, and I've got to keep an eye on her. You could stay out there and keep her from pulling any funny stuff on us."

"If you are so sure she is a murderess, how can you want me to stay alone with her?" Sally's rage had turned to sarcasm.

"Come over here to my office." The receiver clicked in her ear.

"Dick thinks I might go out and stay with the arch-fiend to-night," she informed Andy coldly. "He orders me to come over to his office right away. All right?"

"Lord, yes. Go to it." Andy grinned at her.

Sally called Alice from her brother's office, while he listened over an extension telephone on his stenographer's desk. Alice was cordial; she thanked Sally for calling. Her nerves were much better. No, she thought it better for Sally to go on home and get a night's rest, away from all the excitement.

"Stop by to-morrow afternoon and have a cup of tea with me," said Alice. "If I don't see you before then, I'll need you then, I'm sure. I think I've told your brother everything I know, and if anything else happens, Sally, I'll call you straight away."

"Of course I'll see you to-morrow," said Sally.

"I need a night's rest myself," said Alice. "There is a lot of work ahead of me; if all these officers and newspapermen can't solve this terrible thing"—her voice trembled slightly for the first time—"I think I can and I'm never going to stop trying until I do. I suppose I ought to get a lawyer to advise me. Well, we'll talk about that to-morrow. Good night, honey. You get some sleep, and keep that clever brain polished up for me." She hung up.

Sally looked over at her brother and made a wry face.

"Well, that's that!" he said, disgusted, coming back to his desk. "I suppose I'll have to rely on putting a couple of men out there to watch the house. Miss Blair said she let the nurse go back to Galveston. Well, I'll take a chance she won't fly the coop. Come on, you trusting infant; let's go home. I need sleep and quiet, myself."

"Dick, did you talk to her about the Caruthers statement? You're not talking for publication, now, on my honor."

"Yes, I did. I went out to her apartment this afternoon, just after I gave that statement to the reporters. She was very frank about it—that is, with this brand of frankness she puts out. It looks honest, but I don't believe her; I refuse to believe her."

"You're such a fool, Dick. What did she say?"

"Why, she claims that she spent the six hours driving up and down the Galveston beach and the seawall boulevard. But she can't prove it."

"How do you explain old man Fox?" asked Sally cynically.

"How do you?" countered her brother.

"I don't. I don't explain anything, not even my belief in Alice. I've just got that, and you all can't take it away from me."

8

The girl reporter and the district attorney met at the breakfast table Saturday morning.

"Have you decided what to do about Alice Blair?" Sally asked.

"Sleeping on it didn't help much, honey." Her brother was taking her into his confidence in an unprecedented way.

"It didn't help me, either. But I *know* Alice is innocent. I know it!"

"Well, I'm more or less inclined to agree with you. But before I do anything, I'd like to get my hands on O'Toole. I want that man!"

"So does Alice!"

"I think I'll go out there to see her about eleven o'clock this morning. Maybe you'd better be there; she appears to have confidence in you."

"I'll be there."

At the office, after a hesitation that made him insistent, Sally finally told Rorke about the valentine and the letter she had seen under the box of candy on Alice's desk.

"You nitwit!" Johnny groaned. "You didn't read that letter?"

"I didn't have a chance to read it, Johnny. While I was sitting there looking at it, I was afraid she might come in and catch me at it, and then she waked up and there wasn't a chance. And I clear forgot it later, when I went to bed after she had gone back to sleep."

"There's one room in every house," the star reporter commented dryly, "where you can read forbidden literature."

"Johnny! I'm not so bright, am I?"

There was such genuine contrition in her voice and face that her mentor softened.

"Yes, I reckon you are; you're a right smart kid, Sally. Nobody expects you to learn all the tricks of the trade at once. But when you get back out there, you get that letter!"

"Steal it?"

"Borrow it—without mentioning the loan, innocent!"

He wandered out of the city room. Sally was impatient. After all, maybe that letter would tell something; maybe it wouldn't! The way everybody suspected Alice made her tired!

She looked at her watch: twenty minutes to eleven. She had written the obituary notices and had called the school board and the city federation of clubs. It was time to get back to more interesting work.

"Andy," she said to the city editor, "Dick is going out to see Alice Blair at eleven, and he wanted me to be there when he got there; he thinks maybe she will talk more freely to him with me there. All right?"

"Sure, kid. Better get a move on."

As Sally entered the vestibule of the apartment over Alice Blair's shop, she heard pounding overhead. She ran up the stairs. Her brother and a man she recognized as Dietrich Arnold, a detective on the district attorney's staff, were in the second-floor hall.

"She doesn't answer the telephone nor the doorbell." Lomax growled; plainly he was more than annoyed. "If she has got out of this apartment, there's going to be the devil to pay around here."

"Where's the officer you set to watch her?" Sally asked. Her heart was thumping. Had she been deceived in this girl?

"One's out front and one's at the back. I called her on the telephone, and when she didn't answer, I came straight out. There was no way to reach my men. I didn't want all the people in the apartment to know I had set a watch. Huldy, the officer out front, says there has been no one out of the apartment except the regular tenants since he relieved the night man at seven o'clock this morning."

They had retreated to the hall window. Dick spoke to the detective.

"Arnold, you go find the janitor of this place. I'm going into that apartment!" He thrust his hands into his coat pockets, and began to whistle *"La Golondrina."*

Sally turned from the window, where she had been asking herself troubled questions, as Arnold and the negro janitor clumped up the stairs.

"Got a key that will fit this door, boy?"

"Yassah, yassah, Mr. Lomax, I got a key. I reckon it's all right fo' me to open it fo' you?"

"Certainly it's all right!"

Lomax, followed by Sally, Arnold and the janitor, entered the living-room. It was dusky, for the shades at the front windows were drawn. There was a faint odor of stale tobacco fumes; Sally recognized Alice's Russian cigarettes. Lomax raised the shades, none too gently. To the girl, standing just within the door, there was something depressing in the morning sunshine that came in; some vague unease hovered over these sophisticated furnishings. A rakish pottery lamb, picked out by a beam of sunshine, leered at her from the skyscraper book shelves beside the *chaise longue.*

Dick Lomax had gone from the front windows to the closed bedroom door, prim in its apple-green paint, and was rapping impatiently on it. There was no answer.

"Suppose you go in; she may have drugged herself to sleep again," Dick suggested to his sister. She opened the door.

The curtains at the two windows looking onto the side street were fully drawn. The duplex shades were down tight, too.

"Alice?" Sally called in a small voice. "Alice?" Louder. She waited, her heart beating almost audibly. She could make out the girl's head on the pillow, the eyes open, but unblinking.

Dick and the detective had come in gingerly. Dick, standing uncertain for a minute, crossed to the bed and laid a hand on the white arm stretched out upon the coverlet, just as Arnold let a window shade fly up with a snap.

"Good God!" said the district attorney.

Alice Blair, fully clothed, was lying dead on her dainty green bed. On the rug, beneath her right hand, which trailed toward the floor, was a snub-nosed, blue automatic pistol.

Sally stood very still. So did the district attorney, the detective, the janitor. Finally, her voice as small as when she had called the girl, Sally appealed to her brother.

"She's dead, Dick. Isn't she?"

Lomax nodded. "Several hours. She's—cold."

The voices released Arnold from his respectful silence. He went over close to the bed, and leaned down, careful not to touch anything.

"Quick and clean," he said in a conversational tone. "Right through the roof of the mouth. Out like a light." He snapped his fingers.

Again Lomax nodded. "Well, maybe it was the best way out," he mused aloud. "Poor girl!"

"Yes, sir, I reckon she knew we had the goods on her." Arnold straightened up. "Or else she was afraid of O'Toole."

The janitor had faded quietly from the room. Apparently neither man had noticed his leaving, nor did Lomax pay any heed to his sister, until he heard her voice at the telephone in the living-room.

"No idea just when, Andy," she was saying. "All I know—dead—suicide—pistol near her right hand on the floor at the side of the bed—went through the roof of her mouth—uh-huh—Arnold says it was instant death— Yes— Yes, of course." The receiver rattled back on the hook, and she looked around as Dick almost ran into the room.

"Get away from that phone!"

"Don't be an ass!" It was a relief to let honest anger at her brother rise above the wild thumping of her heart.

He let his rage go, too.

"I tell you, you've got to quit this newspaper nonsense! You're playing hell with my work!"

Sally shrugged her shoulders.

"How could you keep this out of the papers?" she asked coldly. "Do you want me to call Justice Overland?"

"Get away! I'll call him myself!"

"Oh, that's all right. I don't mind." She called the familiar number. "Judge Overland, please. . . . Sally Lomax, of the *Pioneer*. . . . Hello, Judge. . . . Fine, thank you. Listen, can you come out to Alice Blair's apartment?" Her voice faltered slightly. "She has killed herself . . . I said she *killed* herself . . . The district attorney is here. He asked me to call you. . . . Thanks." She hung up hastily.

For a moment she studied the big man glowering at her. Nice old Dick. Dumb, but nice. He would be in a mess again, with her getting the break on this story.

"Here, Dick," she said, rising. "You sit down and call George Monroe and Roscoe Eddy. There's no use in your getting in bad with them again. Won't take you but a minute. Come on, be a lamb. Better call Monroe first; Andy's had time to make the street, almost, as it is."

"So I'm to be a reporter, too." Her brother was nastily sarcastic. "Arnold, will you call the *Record* and the *Bulletin* and tell them about this?" He began pacing up and down the living-room, listening to Arnold's curt reports of the tragedy to the excited newspapermen.

Sally had retreated to the front window to get herself in hand. Could she go back in there and look at that girl again? It was her duty. She moved slowly toward the bedroom as Arnold rose from the desk. Suddenly she felt faint; her legs refused to go on. She sat down on the *chaise longue,* shakily lighted a cigarette, dropped the match into the big brass bowl on the lowest level of the bookcase beside her, glancing down as she let it fall. In the bowl, she noticed absently, were long white pasteboard cylinders, the mouthpieces of Alice Blair's Russian cigarettes. In the bowl, too, was a crumpled ball of blue paper—evidently an envelope. Sally leaned over and picked it up, half smoothed it out. Scrawled on it, in an oddly familiar handwriting, she saw "Alice Bl—."

Lomax and Arnold had gone back into the bedroom; Sally was alone. She crumpled the envelope in her hand and got up; the shakiness had gone from her legs, magically. She crossed swiftly to the desk. Yes, the corn-colored letter that Alice had thrust into the pigeonhole was still there! She barely had stuffed it and the blue envelope into her purse and turned guiltily toward the bedroom door, when her brother and the detective came back into the room.

At that moment the telephone rang, its cheerful jingle making Sally jump away from the desk. Lomax reached for it; hesitated.

"Newspapers," he growled. Sally giggled, almost hysterical with excitement. Her brother took off the receiver.

"This is Miss Blair's apartment," he said testily. "Who is calling? . . . For heaven's sake, what are you calling here

for? This is Dick Lomax . . . What did you want with her?
. . . Well, old man, I'm sorry to tell you, but she killed
herself last night . . . Pistol shot—through the roof of the
mouth . . . Yes, pretty bad . . . No, of course not. Don't
worry about that . . . Sure, see you later. Good-by."

"Who was that?" Sally demanded.

"It was a man who had an appointment with Miss Blair
for ten-thirty this morning at his office. He called to find
out why she hadn't shown up. That's all."

"All right, but who is he?"

"Wouldn't you like to know?" her brother mocked her.
"It's a man who doesn't need notoriety in your paper."

"You *can* be nasty when you try, Dick. Who asked me to
come out here with you? How do you expect to keep any
of this out of the newspapers? Don't be such a complete
ass! Do you want me to print that this call came in and
you refused to tell who it was? I'll print exactly what you
said just now."

"All right, Sally, all right! You're right, I did ask you
to come out here, and I beg your pardon for losing my
temper." He came over and patted her hand. "It was Bob
Morrison; she was going to talk to him about the case this
morning. Did Overland say he would be right out?"

Sally nodded. Lomax turned again to the telephone and
called police headquarters. Briefly he reported what had
happened and said the justice was on his way out to exam-
ine the body. By the time he had done that, the newspapermen had begun to arrive.

Eddy, Monroe and Rorke came within a few minutes of
one another. Sally recognized two or three lesser members
of the *Record* and *Bulletin* staffs. Jesse Martin, the photographer from the *Pioneer,* beat the other photographers
there, as usual. Directed by Rorke, Martin set up his cam-
era in the bedroom. The living-room presently began to
fill with an inrushing cloud of choking flashlight smoke.

Rumbling with rage, eager to vent his suppressed ire on some one, the district attorney strode into the bedroom. A policeman and two more detectives crowded in; there was a clangor in the street as an ambulance arrived. The decent sorrow of Alice Blair's death had been destroyed for Sally—made crass and ugly by men to whom murder and suicide were more impersonal than a baseball score.

Rorke had brought word that Andy wanted her to come in and write her own story for the home edition, so she went slowly down to her car. This meant another by-line; somehow a by-line didn't seem important now. Tears began to roll down her cheeks as she drove, slowly and soberly, through the back streets to the *Pioneer* office.

She meant to learn to be impersonal about tragedy; she had been so when it was Angela Browning's death, but she couldn't be impersonal and professional about the grisly end of this lovely girl who had become almost an old friend in the last three days of life.

"What do you want from me, Andy?" she asked at the city desk. "Just a running story of how the body was discovered, and so on?"

The old man looked at the tear stains about her eyes, and his voice was uncommonly gentle.

"Yeah, in full, kid. You've got an hour. Put it all in; make it as dramatic as you want to; first person. Tell how you happened to be there; everything. Bring in the story of how you slept out there the other night, and tell as much as you want of what she said then. Tell what she told you about her sweetheart, and how she described her sister. You're free to print all that now.

"Jesse!" he bawled as the photographer sauntered in, munching a bar of chocolate candy. "What did you get? Don't stand there! . . . Well, who the hell said you were? Don't argue. I want prints, not oratory. Get out of here!"

Sally, at her desk, took off her hat and pushed back her hair. She rolled three sheets of copy paper into her machine, and sat looking at it, reflectively. What was it Dr. King had always said about simplicity? Keep to Anglo-Saxon; avoid the Latin polysyllables. "Force, in simple Saxon." Funny to think of college lectures in English when she was writing about the suicide of Alice Blair. Alice would have been a grand roommate in college. Sally blew her nose and attacked the keyboard.

"Alice Blair, sister of Angela Blair Browning, the woman found dead in the burned house on Telephone Road Wednesday morning, lay down on her dainty green bed last night and shot herself through the brain," Sally's fingers pecked out slowly.

"Wait a minute."

She jumped. The city editor was reading over her shoulder.

"I wouldn't call that such a hot lead for a story like you've got," he said. "Here, swallow this, kid." He held out a glass of whiskey.

The girl absently took the liquor and gulped it down. The gruff old man smiled as he took back the glass.

"Must have been a shock. But we can't let this story get away from us. Now listen: Johnny is going to put all the spot news in his lead story. What I want you to write is just what you saw in that room; just what you read in that dead girl's face. Especially after what she told you the other night. Not the straight news, you see, but what you know about the inside story of it."

Sally nodded, dumbly grateful. She replaced the spoiled paper, and started over. Her fingers seemed to be released now.

Fifteen minutes later she turned in the first sheet of her story, and was rewarded with Andy's "This is just what

I want, kid. Let it run till you tell all of it." She wrote steadily, calling the copy boy as she finished each page, herself taking the last one to the desk. Andy reached for it, read it hastily, marking the paragraphs with right angles, wrote in one sub-head, and then leaned back.

"Very nice yarn, Sally. Now you race back out to the apartment and see if you can turn up anything the smart boys have overlooked. Better stop downstairs and get something to eat. Don't hurry. We won't extra again to-day on this unless they find O'Toole. I want a new lead for the Sunday city edition. Take your time, kid, and find me one."

The curious were clustered around the street door of the Blair place when Sally stopped her car at the curb. A policeman let her into the vestibule.

"Everybody has gone from up there except Mr. Manning, Miss Lomax," he said. "Sure horrible, ain't it? She was a mighty pretty girl."

Sally nodded.

Manning was poking around in the kitchen. When she called him, he came through the bedroom into the living-room.

"Well, this is a quick end to a good story, ain't it?" The district attorney's chief investigator sat down in one of the low chairs and fished a crumpled packet of cigarettes out of his pants pocket. Sally accepted one.

"Did anybody find anything important here after I left?" she asked.

"Nothing much. I got the gun before anybody touched it. It's wrapped up there on the desk. Thought I'd just look at the prints on it."

It was wrapped, Sally saw, in a yellowed silk handkerchief and lying on the top of the heart-shaped box of candy. She crossed over and looked at it, pushed at it with one finger until it slid off onto a folded copy of the *Bulletin* somebody had left lying beside the box. The contents of the pigeonholes had been pulled out and scattered helter-skelter over the desk; the men reporters had gone through thoroughly. Suddenly she remembered that corn-colored letter in her purse. She didn't know why she hadn't read it. Well, this was no time to begin, with Manning sitting there.

She lifted the top of the candy box. The card which had read "To the Little Copperhead from her Big Rattler" was gone. She had forgotten about it, until now. (Later in the day she was to see that message in a box on the front page of the *Record,* headed "Who is the Rattler?" George Monroe had found one tidbit. Until Monday, every edition of the *Record* insistently asked: "Who is the Rattler?")

Manning reached over and took a chocolate from the box, munching it reflectively.

"This girl shot herself about midnight, I reckon," he remarked. He took another piece of candy, covered with dark red tinsel, and unwrapped it slowly. Sally was fascinated by his hunger for the dead girl's candy, his evident appreciation of it. Two nights before she had eaten from that box with Alice Blair.

"Huldy came on at seven o'clock this morning, and McMullen—he's the man who was on out front during the night—told us the light in the living-room was turned off about twelve. He didn't hear the shot, but that little gun wouldn't make much noise stuck in a person's mouth and on a pillow; not enough for McMullen to hear out on the street. The man out back wouldn't have heard it, anyway. Nobody in the house heard it. But everybody in the house turned in before midnight, they all say." He took another chocolate.

"Is the body still here?"

"Oh, no. Your brother had it taken down to Westheimer's before he and Judge Overland left. Lucky you weren't here. The whole back of her head was blown out."

Sally, wandering uncertainly into the bedroom, stood at the foot of the bed, gazing at the stains on the green silk spread where it covered the pillow. Were suicides always so messy? She felt faint; the room was turning black. She steadied a knee against the rounded foot of the mattress, set her teeth and held her eyelids tight. When she opened them, quickly, at a sound on the bed, Manning, as nonchalantly as he had taken the candies from the box, was tossing the other pillow over the stains.

"Say, I did find something out here in the kitchen," he spoke over his shoulder, impersonally. "Found it in the garbage pail. Come here."

Sally followed his broad back into the shining white kitchen.

"There was a couple of water glasses in the sink," Manning said, "under the hot water faucet, both filled with water. After everybody else left, I looked around. Found this in the garbage can under the sink." He opened a cupboard door over the sink board and showed Sally a pint whiskey bottle.

"Smells like good Bourbon," Manning went on. "At any rate, whether it was Bourbon or not, if she emptied that, she got up plenty of Dutch courage to shoot herself."

"But why the two glasses? Did she have company?"

Manning snorted.

"If anybody had come in and gone out, our boys would have seen him, wouldn't they? She used both of them. She drank the whiskey out of one, took a chaser of water out of the other, turned the hot water into the two glasses in the sink, pitched the empty bottle into the garbage doo-dad, went into the front room, turned out the light, and shot herself after she laid down on the bed. That's the way I got the whole thing doped out. Funny she should be a good housekeeper right up to the last. That's a woman for you."

"Mind if I use your name in that story?"

"I don't know; your brother might raise Ned with me."

"Let him." Sally dismissed the district attorney bluntly. She went back through the death chamber into the living-room, called the *Pioneer* office and asked for the city desk.

"I have a little bit of new stuff, Andy," she began without preamble. "Mr. Manning found an empty pint whiskey bottle in the garbage pail and some glasses in the sink."

"For God's sake, Sally! Ain't there nobody in this office got any brains or luck but you? Hold it a minute."

Johnny's voice came over the wire.

"Yeah?"

"Mr. Manning found an empty whiskey bottle in the garbage pail after you all left, Johnny," she repeated.

"What! Any glasses?"

"Two."

"Two glasses!"

"Yes, but he says she used both of them herself." Sally went on to repeat Manning's explanation of how Alice had fortified herself for the suicide. Then she told what Alice had said of her sister's attitude toward Prohibition.

"This is exclusive, Johnny. Use Manning's name, and I'll keep him from giving it to any one else. He says it was good Bourbon whiskey."

"Wonder where she got it? I'd like to know a bootlegger who could supply good Bourbon. Now I do want O'Toole."

"Don't joke, Johnny. I've got the creeps. I can't believe, even if I saw it myself, that a girl as dainty as Alice Blair would take such a messy way to die. Did you see—the bed?"

"Yes, I saw it. Well, honey, there are few dainty sui-cides, you know. This one is lots nicer than getting sick from poison. Here, talk to Andy."

"Manning got any theory about the motive, Sally?"

"Hold the phone; I'll ask him." But Manning had noth-ing to add to the statement the district attorney had given

Rorke, Monroe and Eddy before he had gone back to his office: there was no apparent motive for the act, unless the dead girl knew something or discovered something that had caused her to kill herself in remorse.

"Why don't your precious brother come out and say he thinks she killed her sister and be done with it?" Andy growled.

"Don't ask me. Do you want me to stay out here?"

"Well, find out if they are going to keep a watch out there for the present, see if anybody knows who will inherit the hospital and the shop, ask what they are going to do about burial—and, oh, yes, jewelry! What sort of jewelry did this girl have?"

"All right."

"I reckon you can come in when you get those things. Sure there's nothing else the bright boys have missed?" Andy knew how to commend a deserving reporter, and right now Sally Lomax was his most deserving.

"I'll see. Thank you, Andy. I'll be in after a while."

She went back to the kitchen, feeling somehow better. She and Manning looked through the drawers of the cabinet, and through the clothes closets, finding nothing unusual. Sally listed the few simple pieces of good, modern jewelry they found in the bedroom. She took casual leave of Manning, intent on her thoughts.

Back at the *Pioneer* office, she wrote briefly an insert for the Sunday editions; and then she and Johnny drifted down for coffee. Johnny mentioned that he and George Monroe had gone through the desk.

"Careful gal, that," he remarked. "Nothing in the desk but receipted light and gas bills and such, and one bill of lading for some dresses coming from New York. I looked for the letter you said was there, but I couldn't find it."

Sally nodded. The letter was in her purse, lying on the table six inches from Johnny's cigarette hand.

"Well, so long, kid," he said, as they strolled up to the door of the Pioneer Building. "I'm off to Galveston on the next interurban. We got a tip from down there that may locate O'Toole, and I want that bozo. I still think he's got the solution to all this."

"It's a shame he didn't get to see Alice before she killed herself." Sally was unusually sober. "She was so terribly in love with him. I don't believe she would have done it if she had talked with him."

"That's why I want to find him; that's why Dick Lomax wants to find him. If she didn't help in the murder of her sister, what made her kill herself—unless she knew that this fellow she loved did it?" Johnny didn't expect Sally to solve these riddles.

"Johnny, I'll tell you something if you won't laugh at me."

Rorke looked at the earnest face, and smiled. "I won't laugh at you, child. What is it?"

"I don't believe Alice Blair killed herself."

"Now, don't go off on that wild idea, Sally." Johnny's voice and face became stern. "No, honey, that was suicide. No woman lays herself down on a bed and lets a murderer shoot her through the roof of the mouth without a struggle. That's hooey. Wait a minute. I'm going upstairs with you."

Johnny conferred with Andy while Sally hung up her hat. She was weary and she didn't know what to do. She went over to the cooler and gulped a cup of water. Johnny, leaving, tossed her a "so long"; Andy bawled "Sally" in the same minute.

"Here, smoke one of my cigarettes for a change," he said. Andy was growing positively chummy. "I think we've got this story about in hand. If the boys turn up O'Toole in Galveston to-night, we'll be set. If they don't, there's nothing to print to-morrow except a re-hash of to-day's stories and an interview with your brother, which I've already got."

"What did you get from Dick?"

"Oh, little enough. Says recent developments—God, why do officials have to use those stale terms—that is to say, the suicide of Alice Blair would indicate that she knew or learned something about the murder of her sister that she didn't tell him when he talked with her Friday afternoon. He thinks she killed herself either in desperation or remorse. She didn't impress him as being heartbroken with grief."

"Does Dick say that? Why, how terrible! That girl was beside herself with grief."

"Like as not, Sally. But you must remember that your brother is a sort of high policeman and policemen are always ready with an alibi for something they aren't sure they can solve. Dick's a good prosecutor, I reckon, but the whole tribe of them are alike: they play safe. Another election is always coming. It's my opinion that none of these officers believes they will lay hands on O'Toole for many a day. They think the case is likely to stay as it is for several months. O'Toole will turn up in some other state a year or two from now, on a bootlegging charge, like as not, and they'll grab him. Johnny thinks this is a hot tip he's out on now, but I haven't got much faith in it. But you call it a day. I don't think there is much else you can do, and you look all petered out. Run along home, and be down bright and early Monday morning."

"I don't like to go if there is anything you need me for."

"Nope. Don't need you for a thing now. If I do, I'll give you a ring." Andy's feet went up on the desk; he hitched his hat onto the back of his head; it was his way of going into conference with himself.

Sally gathered up half a dozen copies of the noon and home editions, told an office boy to save her a couple of the final, and started home. She would clip out those stories, take a bath, play with the cat, talk to Lulu, and be a lady, she would.

Dick had telephoned the housekeeper he would not be home for dinner, Lulu reported.

"Said as he was goin' to drive down to Galveston, Miss Sally."

So Dick had the same tip Johnny had. Oh, well, she was weary of the whole thing. She wanted to forget it. She did forget it while she bathed and washed her hair; dressed leisurely. She went downstairs to the library to clip her newspapers, going about it with a certain virtuous satisfaction. She must send some of these signed stories to the girls in the sorority. What a kick they would get out of her writing about an actual murder! And such a murder! She even considered sending a set of them to Dr. King. He would be so shocked! Well, it *was* shocking.

Just then the letter came to her mind. Why hadn't she read that letter? Or told Johnny about taking it? She opened her purse, which she had brought down with the roll of newspapers. Out of it tumbled the crumpled blue envelope on which she had seen "Alice Blair"; which she had entirely forgotten. The full inscription, in blue ink and hard to make out, brought her up in her chair.

"*To be opened by my sister, Alice Blair, in the event of my sudden death.*"

Sally's hands shook. Angela had written this and died; Alice had read it and died; here was the envelope; where was the ominous message it had held?

There was no fireplace in Alice's apartment where she could have burned the letter. The garbage pail in which Manning had found the empty whiskey bottle was the only receptacle for trash, except the empty waste basket in the living-room. Maybe Alice had torn it up and sent it down the sewer. Then why hadn't she put the envelope there, too?

"In the event of my sudden death."

Angela Browning had feared sudden death—the death that had finally overtaken her!

All at once Sally found herself longing for Johnny Rorke; wishing that she had shown him that envelope. Why had she forgotten it? She even wished for her brother. Why did both of them have to go off to Galveston?

Trembling, out of the purse she took the corn-colored envelope. The writing on it was patently by the same hand that had addressed the blue envelope; that was no surprise; Angela had posted the letter in Galveston on Tuesday; Alice would have received it in the afternoon a few hours before she and Mrs. Caruthers started to Galveston.

Angela's attack was direct:

> "Dear Alice:
> "Let me warn you again about running around with the wrong man. *Cut it out!* I know just how a girl's life can be ruined by bad judgment. I know how easy it is to fall in love with a handsome man who can make pretty speeches.
> "I'm not saying this man is not a square shooter. I know he is. He is, also, a fine person in many ways, but he is a jailbird and a lawbreaker and no good can come to you from associating with him. Besides, he is beneath you in every way; his education, his breeding, his past are all wrong for you. You will be miserable if you fall in love with him.
> "I don't want you to think I am throwing things up to you or reminding you of past favors, but I have worked too hard and too long for you, and I've put in too much to see

my investment go bad. Now stop this while you can. *I mean this.*

"I want to say more than that. I've helped too many unmarried girls, who come dragging here to me. I've seen too many deserted wives. I know what it means. I know these men with their fair promises and their dirty double-crossing. It's just as bad to have to work with a husband in prison, as it is to have to work after one has run off and left you. A man who has no respect for the law will have no regard for a wedding ceremony, either. He may not consider one necessary. And I have no intention of standing around with a shotgun in my hand, *while I watch my sister get married so she can give a name to her child!*

"I love you very dearly, but I won't tolerate any nonsense. Get that straight!

"Sister."

Sally, lighting a cigarette, glowered at the two envelopes and the sheet of paper. Just what did all this mean?

After all, did O'Toole kill that woman? Alice had described her sister as the "red-headedest woman" she had ever known. Had Angela flown into a rage after Terry had talked to Alice over the phone? Possibly. Had she called him a jailbird and told him he was beneath Alice? Probably. Had she overplayed her hand, threatening O'Toole? It was hard to accept that as a motive for murder by a man as suave as Alice had implied O'Toole was. But where was any motive in this crazy mess? A man, drunk, in a rage, might shoot or stab; but poison? No. Poison meant premeditation, if Sally knew her detective stories. No one would give a man and a woman a lethal dose of morphine in anger or sudden rage. That was out.

Where did old man Fox fit into the picture? Why had he died in the room, with the key broken off in the door? If he had strength enough left to break a key, why hadn't he strength enough to get out by the back door? Who had blocked that back door? . . . Where is Terry O'Toole? . . . Alice believes he didn't have a! thing to do with the murder—that is, Alice did believe that.

Sally shivered; vividly before her had come that stained green silk coverlid, the strands of red hair dried in the blood. Why should Alice have killed herself? That letter from Angela— in the blue envelope—what had that told? Where had Alice put it?

Sally could hear Lulu talking at the telephone, but she paid no attention to what was being said. She wanted some one to help her work out this puzzle; wondered if it would do any good for her to call up Manning and ask him to come out. But no. Manning didn't share her belief that Terry O'Toole had nothing to do with the murder and fire on Telephone Road. Nobody credited the bootlegger's innocence but herself. She sat gazing into the fire, weary of thinking.

The doorbell rang. She heard Lulu padding down the long hallway.

"Yes, sir, Miss Sally's at home. Come right in; she's right in there in the liberry."

Sally looked up impatiently. Lulu had such informal ways; she seldom thought to ask if Sally wanted to see a visitor.

A tall man was standing in the doorway; well-dressed, but disheveled; handsome, but haggard. His blue eyes glowed vividly from burned-out sockets.

"You are Miss Lomax—Miss Sally Lomax?" he asked warily.

She nodded. "Yes, I am Sally Lomax."

"May I come in and talk to you? I am Terence O'Toole."

9

Sally, very still at the big table, Angela Browning's letter spread out before her, studied O'Toole with an odd detachment. That he should have walked in so casually, so easily, while she had sat there saying to herself, "Alice didn't believe he did it," was doubtless amazing; but she wasn't really surprised. She had needed help, and it had walked in.

"Sit—sit—down, won't you?" It was only when she had to speak that she realized how startled she was.

"Thank you." O'Toole put his hat on a chair near the door, stood uncertain for a moment, then took off his overcoat, and put it under the hat. He came over and sat down in a chair near the table. Sally noticed his lanky grace. He was rather personable for a bootlegger. But then Alice Blair had had good taste in other things; why shouldn't the man she had loved be rather above the ordinary?

"I'm glad to find you at home, Miss Lomax," O'Toole said, interlacing his long, strong fingers. "I telephoned to the *Pioneer* office and asked for you, but they said you had gone home for the day. When I phoned out here your maid told me you were alone, so I just came on out."

"Why did you want to see me?"

"Alice trusted you, didn't she? I know that from the stories you wrote about her. After I read the afternoon

papers"—he cleared his throat—"I had to talk to somebody, and it seemed to me you were the only one I could
trust."

Sally smiled, nervously.

"I was going to your brother and give myself up,"
O'Toole went on, slowly, "but after I read that story of
yours again about—finding Alice on her bed, I decided
I'd rather talk to you than to him. I knew you were the
district attorney's sister; the folks I have been staying with
told me that. Is he here?" He glanced quickly at the doors.

Sally laughed, and Sally's laugh was the sort that made
others join in.

"He went to Galveston on a 'hot tip' that he would find
you there to-night," she said.

The man, in spite of his grave eyes, laughed with her.
It broke the skein of embarrassment. Sally held out a box
of cigarettes. O'Toole took one, snapped on his lighter for
hers.

"I haven't been in Galveston since Wednesday noon,"
he said. "I read the first extras that day at breakfast, and
started right up to Houston to see Alice. But she beat me
here. On the way through town, I bought another paper, a
later one, while my car was held up by the lights on Main
Street. That one told me that Angela had been identified.
I knew I'd be the first one they looked for after they knew
it was Angela. So I ducked. And I stayed—right here in
Houston. I haven't been out of the city limits since."

"How did you get out here?"

"Drove out. With the license plates changed, my car
is just like thousands of other black sedans. I drove right
along and walked in. None of the smart detectives is going
to look for me in the district attorney's home." He chuckled sarcastically. "Besides, what have I got to worry about
now? I don't give one good damn what happens. I haven't
got anybody to protect."

"Whom were you protecting before?" Sally's heart was racing.

"Alice. I didn't want her or other people to know that her sister was a bootlegger—and they will find that out as soon as they put me on the witness stand."

"What—what did you say?"

"I said Angela Browning was bootlegging. I ought to know; she was my partner. Where do you suppose she got all the money she spent? Not out of a hospital where half the patients were charity cases. How much do you suppose she was worth when she died? Nearly a hundred thousand—and in good bonds, at that."

"Mercy me alive!"

"Oh, she was pretty smart, Angela was. Even if she wasn't smart enough to keep from drinking doped whiskey. The hell cat!" He fell into a silence, looking down at his fingers, locked and twisting between his knees. When he lifted his eyes, he looked at Sally, appraisingly.

"You're a lot younger than I thought you'd be," he decided. "Those things you wrote about Alice sounded like you were years older than she was. But I reckon you're all right, even if you are so young and the D.A.'s sister. But you want to know why I've come out here?"

Sally said nothing.

"I want to get the man who made Alice kill herself."

"What do you mean by that?"

"I mean that the man who killed Angela made Alice kill herself. *I want that man.* If I can't choke the life out of the rat, I want to know the law will." O'Toole's blue eyes looked green, and his black hair seemed vibrant with the passion in his voice. "I can't do one thing in this town by myself. I know that. I'm wanted, I'm suspected, and I'll be arrested the minute an officer gets a sight of me. But, Miss Lomax, my arrest won't solve this hellish thing. Oh, they may be able to fasten it on me; I haven't got one earthly soul to prove I wasn't out at that dump on Telephone Road that night when the fire started. I was there before it started. I've been in jail. I make my living by breaking a damn' fool law. They may be able to fasten it on me. I won't be the first innocent man who has been railroaded to the pen or the chair to clear an official's record! But, Miss Lomax, I didn't do it. The man who did do it was responsible for Alice's—death—*and I want that man!*"

Sally asked him calmly: "Who is he, Mr. O'Toole?"

"God, if I only knew! Do you suppose if I knew who did it I would be here? By God, he would have been dead at two o'clock this afternoon. It doesn't take long to fill a skunk full of lead. Listen, I'm going to tell you all about this thing from the beginning. Do you mind? I think if I can talk it out logically, maybe I'll get somewhere; all I've been doing is thinking about one angle of it and then another, until I'm almost crazy. All the time afraid to talk to Alice on the telephone for fear they'd catch me and bring worse sorrow on her. She would never admit even to me that her sister was not the saint those little tarts down in Galveston thought she was. I couldn't talk to the folks I was staying with; it wasn't fair to them to let them know too much. Police officers aren't very polite to the friends of a man suspected of murder—friends who have been hiding him.

"I've been running liquor from ships in Galveston and along the Ship Channel for more than two years, now. That old house on Telephone Road was my depot. We dug a cellar under the house where we stored the stuff. We never sold it on the premises; too risky. I don't think there is much stuff out there now; I had it about cleaned out last week, and I came up here, the night before the fire, to make arrangements with old man Fox for another load to come in this week-end. I think there's about a case of good Bourbon out there, but that's all. That Bourbon was not sold much. It's bonded warehouse stuff. We kept that for special customers and presents.

"When I got out of jail two years ago, I was sick and broke. Somebody told me that Angela Browning would let me in her hospital; that I could be taken care of in the medical ward, away from her maternity cases, and that I could pay her when I got the cash. I went out there and she took me in. When I was well, she gave me two hundred and fifty dollars to stake me, and asked no questions. She was pretty damn' decent, in a lot of ways. I was grateful to her." He lingered a moment over that.

"So when I got a chance to make a connection with some sailors for regular deliveries of good stuff, and I needed cash to swing it, I went to her and asked her to lend me more money. I'd already paid back what I owed her and the hospital, and I knew my credit was good. She asked me what I wanted the jack for, and I told her; everybody in Galveston knows she could keep a closer mouth than all the clams in the ocean. She asked me to let her come in with me; she would furnish the capital to start with, and I could make the connections and handle the business, and we'd split the profits fifty-fifty. It seemed fair enough to me, especially as she dug up this old man Fox and we could use him to make deliveries when I wasn't up here in Houston. Nobody here knew him; she had known him back in Longleaf.

"You see, Alice was coming home, and Angela wanted money to start her out in the shop, and besides she wanted more bonds to put away for her daughter."

"For her *what?*"

"Her kid. Angela has a daughter; none of you knew that, did you? Huh! There's a lot people don't know, and likely won't know, about that woman. The kid is about fourteen now, I reckon. Angela kept her up in Virginia in a swell girls' school. She went up there every summer for a month and stayed with the kid. I always had a hunch the girl was illegitimate; anyway, she never risked having her down here."

"My goodness!"

"Alice didn't know about that kid, either, as far as I know. At any rate, she never let on to me. I'm pretty sure she didn't know about it. Well, anyway, to go on with the story, Angela and I made plenty. Good and plenty. I've got more money in the bank than I ever thought I'd have. I learned from one conviction what to do and what not to do in bootlegging, and there's plenty of profit in it if you know the ropes.

"Last Monday night Angela found out that Alice and I were—you know—in love with each other, and the hell she raised! I don't know how she found it out; Alice hadn't told her, and I hadn't. Anyway, she called me up, but I was too busy to see her that night and she didn't get a chance at me until I started up here on Tuesday night, and she just announced she was coming along. And then what a stink she raised! She spent twenty-five of the fifty miles up here from Galveston giving me unshirted hell, and the rest of the way telling me why she hated men. I knew I'd have to face her music sooner

or later, but I don't mind telling you I got sick of listening to it before we hit League City.

"It seems some guy had ruined her girlhood, and she was determined that Alice should make a safe and sane marriage, if she got married at all. Said she didn't want Alice to marry until she got old enough to know what she was doing, but she supposed she wouldn't be able to keep her from it. I'll say she couldn't; plenty of men want to marry a girl as sweet and fine as Alice."

He leaned over and took another cigarette, lighted it with fumbling fingers, and went on.

"She told me what a hell of a life she led after her baby was born, and how hard she worked to keep the kid clothed and fed, and how she had to work harder after her mother died and she had Alice on her hands. I'll hand that to Angela; she was a damn' good sister to Alice. Not many can do for a kid sister what she did. She said she thought I was pretty decent, but after all, I'd been a jailbird, and she wanted something better than that for Alice. I just laughed at her. I told her I had enough money to go to California and be a banker if I wanted to. But she raved until we got to Houston. She said she was coming up to raise hell with a certain party. 'I'll bet he wishes I was dead,' she said to me. I believed her. 'And if you lay a hand on my sister, you'll wish it had rotted first,' she said. I about believed that.

"We drove on out to old Fox's house and fixed up about this load of booze that is supposed to come in to-night. I reckon that's the tip your brother got in Galveston. Somebody talked. That reward the state and city offered for me ain't bad money for squealing. They think they'll get me at that boat. Well, they're all wet. I got a code radio off to the captain Thursday and that booze is in Davy Jones' locker. That's one boat that will come in dry, and there ain't many dry in this port." He grinned, nervously.

"But anyhow, we fixed up the routine of how this stuff was to be handled. Old Fox was about half lit when we got out there; he'd been drinking whiskey sours. Angela had a couple, I know. I don't drink. I got caught three years ago because I was trying to deliver a load of booze while I was half shot, and I came out of that jail the best personal prohibitionist in these states, I'll tell the world. We sat around and talked and laughed at old Fox and his crazy philosophy, and finally Angela asked Fox why the other party didn't show up. Fox said he wouldn't come in while my car was outside. So Angela told me to clear out, and she'd come home on the interurban. The last thing she said was for me to keep away from Alice.

"So I drove straight on down to Alice's place," O'Toole continued, making no attempt to be funny. "She wasn't there, and then I recollected that she had said she might drive down to Galveston with Mrs. Caruthers and put her on the boat the next day. About eleven-thirty, I put in a call for the Galvez and got Alice. That's the conversation the phone girl told this Rorke about. She listened, all right! She had a good memory, too."

"I know that." Sally smiled at him. "Alice told me all about it, before she saw it in the paper. It checked with the telephone girl's story, exactly."

"Did she tell you? She sure trusted you! Well, I thought of going back to see if Angela's friend had gone, and take her back to Galveston with me. But I didn't want to listen to her rave for another two hours, and she didn't expect me to come, anyway, so I just went on by myself. I got home about two-thirty, and half an hour later Alice drove in."

Sally felt a little shiver run up her spine. So that was where Alice had gone on her midnight drive! Of course!

"I had just put my car into the garage, so I got in hers and we drove up and down the beach and talked until after five o'clock. Then she dropped me off at my house and went on to the hotel. I never saw her or talked to her after that." O'Toole leaned over and crushed out his cigarette almost savagely.

"I was pretty well worn out, and I went right off to sleep and slept like a log. I waked up around noon, dressed and drove uptown to my regular place to eat breakfast. I was sitting there when the waiter brought me over the papers, and I read about the fire and that they thought it was Alice's body. I was knocked so cold at first I couldn't think. And then I realized it must be Angela, because Alice had been in Galveston with me when the fire happened. I beat it down to the pier, but the steamer had already sailed and I knew Alice was likely on her way back to Houston. Like I told you, I started after her, but she had too much start on me. I stopped in Harrisburg and tried to phone her, but she didn't answer, and then I got the later paper, and knew they would connect me with Angela pretty quick. For one thing, I knew that old parrot at the drawbridge had seen me and had seen her. So I came on in to some friends the law don't connect me with. I never did dare phone Alice after that, as I told you, because I didn't want her to find out about her sister's bootlegging, and because I didn't want my friends in bad with the cops. I don't wish anybody bad luck with cops. All they know how to do is hound a fellow. Then I saw about Alice in the papers to-day, and I couldn't sit still any longer, and here I am."

O'Toole slumped back in his chair, waiting for Sally's comments. She felt as though she were in a theater; all this was a fantastic play. Terence O'Toole, for whom they would pay five hundred dollars, had been sitting there rehearsing his part.

What characters the drama had: a bootlegging angel of mercy, a gentle mother and an unselfish sister, the "red-headedest woman"; a bootlegger with a broad streak of chivalry and only occasional lapses in grammar; the lovely little sister, who must be protected, who had acquired her sophisticated tastes in Paris; the old woman hater who was buying a hog farm; the "certain party" Angela had come up to "raise hell" with, who "wished her dead."

Sally flicked the ash from her cigarette and leaned back. She had been bent forward listening so intently that she hadn't realized how tense her nerves, her muscles were. When she spoke, it was with the impulsive girl uppermost, not the cool reporter.

"Mr. O'Toole, I believe that story!" Once she had said it, she felt that it had sounded very young.

In spite of his troubles, his sorrows, and the strain under which he had been living for the past few days, O'Toole grinned.

"It's true enough, Miss Lomax," he protested wryly. "But I don't expect your brother will believe it; lawyers and officials don't like to believe what they don't want to believe."

"What do you mean to do now? What do you want me to do?"

"Help me catch the man back of this."

"How? Who is he?"

"I don't know. If I thought the police wouldn't torture me half crazy, so a 'confession' could clear their skirts, I'd go down to the station and surrender. But they'd bring out the old rubber hose and the high-powered light and the little flicks with the handkerchief."

Sally shut her eyes. She knew about those refinements: the beating with rubber hose that left no bruise or welt; the high-powered light burned steadily at a prisoner's eyes until he was frantic; the incessant, baffling flicks with a handkerchief that wore out the strongest nerves with the simplicity of the torment. The confessions these methods sometimes wrung from innocent men!

"Dick has gone to Galveston. If he has gone out to that boat, he won't be back until midnight."

O'Toole nodded.

"I don't know what to do about it by myself. Maybe the best thing I can do is call in somebody I trust."

"Go the limit, Miss Lomax. I'm trusting you."

Sally went out to the hall telephone and called Andy Hunt at the office.

"What's up, kid? . . . Come out to your house? On Saturday night? . . . I don't get you, Sally. . . . Is it about the Blair case? There's nothing important on that except O'Toole, now . . . Wa-a-it a minute! Don't say another word over this phone! . . . Who the hell do you think I'd want to bring with me?" He was gone.

Sally went from the telephone to the kitchen, where she gave Lulu instructions to set out a light supper for three on the dining-table. Then she returned to O'Toole.

"I've asked Andy Hunt, my city editor, to come out here," she announced. "You can trust Andy, and if he decides for you to surrender, you can depend on it that he won't let anybody try any third-degree stuff."

O'Toole simply looked at her. It dawned on Sally now that the man was physically worn out; that his nerves had let down so that he was ready to depend on her like a child; that his resources of self-control had been drained by those four days of staying away from Alice Blair, and that Alice's death had taken the last of it.

"By the way, Mr. O'Toole," she asked, "do you know who it was Alice called the 'Big Rattler'?"

"That looked silly in the paper, didn't it?" He was blushing. "Those were just our pet names for each other: Little Copperhead and Big Rattler."

The doorbell rang just as Lulu announced that she had cold meats and a salad on the table, whenever Miss Sally wanted to come in. Lulu opened the street door. Sally, just behind her, was a bit flustered. Her home had welcomed many important guests; the Governor had dined there with Dick and her a few weeks before; yet she had never scrutinized the dignified old hallway as critically as now, when her city editor entered it. But Hunt did not even wait to look around him.

"Do you know where O'Toole is?" he demanded.

"Come in, Andy. I asked you to come out and have a bite of supper with me. We'll be there in just a minute or two, Lulu." The cook padded off to the dining-room;

once she was out of hearing, Sally answered. "Come in the library, Andy. I want you to meet Mr. O'Toole."

Hunt threw his hat onto the big chair in the hallway, and followed Sally. By God, he had taken this girl for a society dumb-bell! Wanted to fire her! Suppose he had! Good Lord! The fervor of his relief that he hadn't fired her made his handclasp warm and friendly to O'Toole. Then Sally led the way to the dining-room.

The big silver coffee pot was full; Sally had told Lulu she needn't bother any more; to run along to her Saturday night church meeting. Until the housekeeper had gone, Hunt held his questions.

Sally suggested that O'Toole repeat to Andy the story as he had told it to her. She prompted him here and there; by the time they had finished their meal, the city editor had gathered all the facts she knew. Andy had said very little during the recital; Sally recalled that he was the best poker player on the *Pioneer* staff. When the story was done, the editor had his comment ready.

"I'll not say, O'Toole," he spoke slowly, "that I believe all you have told me. I'd be a fool to say that, when I haven't checked any of the facts. Besides, it's not my business to say whether it's so or not. I'll say it's a good story; too good to print if it is true. Because, if you didn't kill Angela Browning, to print all this story will tip off the man who did. If you did kill her, you're just a killer, and it's not my business to help you frame a publicity yarn that will give your bootlegging friends ample information to fix up your alibi. Half a dozen men, like as not, rode back to Galveston with you that night!" He grinned amiably.

"Now, you can't surrender to the police without getting Dick Lomax's dander up. You'd better give up to him, personally, and I'll see that Dick don't let them work you out. He won't be here until midnight, but if you'll place yourself in my hands, I'll fix the whole thing. I want the story of the surrender, exclusive."

It didn't really matter to O'Toole. He wondered, dully, why he had bothered to come out here and tell all this. Alice was dead. He should have shot himself like she did. She had argued with him once about suicide. Seemed to have an idea that nobody had a right to kill himself. But she had done it. No, she couldn't have! Little Alice, with the dimples and the laugh and the child's trust in him! She couldn't have shot herself!

"I've already put myself in your hands, Mr. Hunt," he said. "I've told Miss Lomax that all I want is the man who killed Angela; he's responsible for Alice's death. If my surrender will help, let's go. If it will do more good for me not to surrender, what do I do next? I can't figure any more."

"Well, I think the best thing is for us to run a story saying that you surrendered to the *Pioneer,* and that we have turned you over to the district attorney. We won't turn you over until four o'clock in the morning. No, wait! We'll let Dick have you at six o'clock. I don't want to give the opposition a chance to make over, after our regular edition is on the press, and they're likely to do that if they find out at four o'clock that you're in the county jail. They can have what they want on Monday morning; we should worry after our first story. One more thing: you're to tell this story you have told Sally and me to *no one!* I want that promise."

O'Toole readily agreed. Andy rose.

"All right, my boy. Let's be off; it's eight o'clock. I'll take you down to the Rice Hotel and let you get a night's sleep there, after we have made some pictures of you. Come on, Sally, let's go."

So, presently, a room was engaged at the Rice Hotel in the name of Andy Hunt, and the city editor and "one of my reporters," with a hat over his eyes, apparently drowsy, went up in the service elevator to it. There the wearied bootlegger tumbled into bed. A reporter, left on watch, was to rouse him at six o'clock and take him to the *Pioneer* office through the back streets.

Through the night Sally stayed at the office with Andy. At six o'clock, she was sitting beside him and Johnny Rorke when Andy called the Lomax house. Rorke had come back from Galveston at one o'clock in the district attorney's car; Dick had dropped him at the *Pioneer* office as he went home. Rorke, after news of O'Toole's surrender to Sally, which had, as he said, left him limp at such luck, had stretched out on the file table to sleep until six.

The district attorney answered the phone sleepily.

"Lomax, this is Andy Hunt, at the *Pioneer*. Can you come down?"

"What's the idea?"

"I want to turn Terence O'Toole over to you; he has surrendered to the *Pioneer*."

Calmly Lomax said: "Very well, Hunt. At your office? I'll be down as soon as I can dress."

When Lomax arrived, he saw, sitting at Andy Hunt's desk, O'Toole on one side of her, Rorke and two reporters on the other, his ubiquitous sister. She looked neither more righteous nor more triumphant than the others, but the mere fact that she was there kindled Lomax's fury against the whole lot of them. Andy, wise old man, saw Lomax stiffen. Before the district attorney could speak, Andy stood up.

"Good morning, Dick. Thanks for coming down. This is Terence O'Toole. He surrendered to the *Pioneer* at six o'clock last night. We are turning him over to you with the plain understanding that he is not to be put through any third degree, that he can have counsel, and that the *Pioneer* can have access to him at all times."

"How do you do, O'Toole. That's agreeable to me, Hunt. May I use your phone?" He ignored his sister entirely. Sally's eyes were dancing.

"That phone is not connected, Dick. Use this one." She pushed Andy's private phone towards him. He glared at her, picked up the phone, and called the county jail.

"Hello, Randy! This is Lomax. I'm bringing a prisoner over."

That was all. Sally looked at her brother's perfectly tailored back for a minute, and then went over to O'Toole, who was standing hesitantly in the middle of the city room floor.

"Good-by, Mr. O'Toole." Her voice was cordial. "I'll get Andy to fix everything up. Oh, wait one minute! Andy! Mr. O'Toole hasn't a lawyer yet. We forgot that!"

"Never mind, O'Toole. I'll call Bob Morrison as soon as I think he's awake. I reckon you have enough money for him, haven't you? We find him pretty high-priced talent."

"Plenty of money, Mr. Hunt. Thank you. Thank you, Miss Lomax."

"That's right, Bob is the *Pioneer's* lawyer." Lomax spoke up. "Oh, all right. Come on, O'Toole."

He went out with the bootlegger, Rorke and the reporter who had stayed in the hotel room with O'Toole trailing after.

Andy Hunt and Sally left the *Pioneer* office together, in broad daylight. Andy had asked Sally if she wanted to go out to the old house on Telephone Road with him to see if they could find the cache O'Toole had said was under the house.

"I'm inclined to agree with you, Sally," he conceded as they got into Sally's roadster, "that this guy is telling the truth. But one of the first things Morrison will want to know is how much we have done to check up on it. Bob is not going to want to fool with this case, with his campaign

for governor coming along so soon; but I reckon he'll have
to look into it, anyway, if I ask him to. It's been too much
of a *Pioneer* story for him to throw it over. He's going to
kick about defending a bootlegger because of the preacher
and woman vote, but we'll make him sit in, and suggest a
trial lawyer."

"One of those men in his firm could take it," Sally said,
"and he wouldn't have to have the publicity."

"Yeah; he'll probably want Potts to take it. Bob is for-
ever choking that guy down my throat. I don't like him;
I distrust him; I think he's crooked." Sally wondered at
Andy's vehemence; he seldom expressed likes and dislikes
so warmly. "I asked Bob once why he kept him around. It
seems that Potts was in Bob's office in Dallas, and trailed
after him down here, and Bob, like the good old fool that
he is, took him into the firm. Oh, well!" Andy sighed,
and spat over the side. "They've made a lot of money, but
that's no credit to Potts!"

There was no guard standing now over the wreck of the
old house. Public curiosity had died out. The sun was just
coming up as Sally parked her car at the gate and followed
Andy up the graveled walk. He looked closely at the blackened
shell of a front door, at the place where Martin Fox's body
had lain; he merely put his head into the room where Angela Browning's body had been found. Andy seldom visited
such places; he had reporters to do the sightseeing for him.

"For a good-looking woman, she sure picked out a
dump to die in, didn't she?" He grunted. "Well, where is
this closet, kid?"

Sally led the way to the closet under the stairs, in
which, the morning after the fire, she had discovered the
kerosene-soaked papers.

"O'Toole said the trap door here opens from the side,
and you have to hunt for the way to open it," she remarked. "Wait until I run back to the car for a flashlight."

They found a round hole in the wall, from which a knot in the grain of the wood had been punched out. Slipping a finger through it, Sally lifted a wooden latch, and pulled out the side of the closet, which swung on hinges, revealing steps which the man and the girl gingerly descended. The cellar was unexpectedly large, with a dirt floor and rough boarded walls. On a pine table against the farther wall stood an oil lantern. Andy struck a match and lighted it. Piled in a corner were empty gunny sacks; one of another heap proved to have half a dozen straw-jacketed bottles in it. Andy pulled out a quart bottle and read aloud the label.

"Well, if this stuff hasn't been cut, I'll say they kept good Bourbon for their pets. Sally, child, this is one time I'm believing in 'finders keepers.'" Andy smacked his lips in anticipation. "I must say this bears out pretty well what the boy said. He may be telling a straight story." His eyes twinkled.

They searched every corner, but there was nothing more to be found. Finally they went back to the car, Andy with a bottle in each overcoat pocket and two clutched to his chest, while Sally held two under her coat. She let Andy out at his house, and drove home, more weary than she cared to admit to herself. Half an hour after she had closed the garage door behind her car, she was sound asleep. She slept until two o'clock Sunday afternoon.

She met Dick at the dinner-table at three o'clock. Apparently he had slept off a good part of his bad temper. Once more he seemed glad to take her into his confidence.

"That was a nice piece of work, Sister," he conceded, as he pulled out her chair for her. "Rorke says you carry a rabbit's foot. I expect that your friend O'Toole is going to need to borrow it before this is over."

"Why?"

"Well, I don't know what his story to you is, but it is going to have to be mighty good for a jury to believe him.

I'll shoot it full of holes, and I haven't even started oiling my guns."

"Maybe so, Dick. But I have a hunch he'll never come to trial."

"Yeah, I know you and your friend Andy think he's innocent, but that's just what *you* think. That's not what a jury of hard-headed men is going to think; the State of Texas doesn't allow newspaper men and women on its juries."

"Did Judge Morrison take the case?"

"Oh, yes, Bob couldn't do anything but take it, after Hunt asked him to. Bob will drop it or turn it over to somebody in his office. Potts, likely."

"Do you like Potts?"

"Why ask me that? What's that got to do with the case?"

"Oh, nothing. I just wondered if you liked him. Andy doesn't."

"Well, you know, Sally, that Hunt chap of yours is a funny guy. I don't make him out all the time. Did you know that yesterday afternoon he arranged for an autopsy on the Blair girl?"

Sally shook her head.

"Yes, sir, he got an autopsy order without bothering to say anything to me about it. I don't see what he expects to find, but since he was paying for it, I didn't make any fuss. There were no relatives to object."

10

Sally and her brother left the dining-room arm in arm. As they were turning into the library, the doorbell rang. Dick went to the door.

"District Attorney Lomax?" asked a youth in uniform. "Special Delivery, sir."

Dick signed the register, and with the letter in his hand, went into the library.

"Nothing but a crank letter, evidently," he pronounced, scanning it. "A crank who has a hunch on the Blair case, I'll bet a hat." He opened the letter. "Mm—hm. I thought so. Here, you'll be more interested in it than I am." He tossed it to Sally.

The letter was written on blue-lined tablet paper; the address on the cheap envelope was in pencil, as was the message inside:

> "You think your so smart you officers arresting that bootlegger he never killed that woman and old man   a dope did it old Fox was just a dope even if he was the best peddler in Houston."

At the bottom of the page, there was an added word: "Airplane."

"What does it mean, Dick?"

"Oh, it's just the first of the smart tricks O'Toole's bootlegger friends will be pulling. I'll get plenty of those in the next week. Always do, you know, and they never amount to anything."

"Don't you investigate anonymous letters, ever?"

"Good heavens, if I did, I'd have to have two extra men on the force doing nothing but that," Lomax answered, picking up the Sunday edition of the *Pioneer*. "I have a hard enough time getting enough money out of the county to pay for the men I work to death. I certainly have none left over for wild goose chases."

"Well, Andy says he never fails to investigate every anonymous letter that comes to his desk, and sometimes he gets two or three in a day," Sally remarked, full of pride. "He says he lost a good story once in New Orleans when he worked on the *Picayune* because he didn't investigate a letter, and he took an oath that he would always look up every tip. He says it's only common sense."

"Yeah? Well, your Andy is smart, no doubt."

"You're right, he is," Sally snapped.

Getting nothing from her brother but a grin over the top of his paper, she folded the note and put it back in its envelope.

For the next hour she and her brother read, silently, the morning papers, which she had not seen and he had had time to scan but briefly. At five o'clock he left the house, saying he was to meet Bob Morrison at the Houston Club.

"Having supper here?" he asked.

"I don't know, Dick. Are you?"

"Probably not. Bob and I expect to drive down to Galveston. I guess we'll have some seafood down there, somewhere."

After her brother had gone, Sally wandered about the house, disconsolate. She browsed further through the papers;

she tried a new novel; it bored her. Finally she called the
Pioneer office. To her great relief, Andy answered.

"Come down and gossip with me and Johnny, if you've
nothing better to do," he invited cordially. More evi-
dence of her acceptance into their male and inky world;
she whistled a tune as she backed her roadster out of the
garage and spun lazily up Waugh Drive and along the bank
of Buffalo Bayou in the misting rain.

She found the men sitting, feet propped up on the radi-
ator, chairs tilted back against Andy's desk, in the other-
wise deserted city room.

"Pull up a chair and set," Hunt said. "You look a little
fresher than you did."

"If the Blair case has many more night sessions, the cub
reporter's going on the blink," Johnny offered sagely.

"Has the unknown man, the mystery man, the guy
Angela came up to raise hell with, called you yet?" Sally
knew that Andy was "giving her the razz," but she didn't
mind. "No? Look here, we can't have that! It's been almost
twenty-four hours since you brought in a prisoner or a
clew. You'd better get busy. You're a hell of a reporter."

"Sunday is supposed to be my day off, Andy. I've got
nothing but an anonymous letter to give you this afternoon. It came Special Delivery to Dick out at the house.
He says it's the bunk, but I thought maybe you'd like to
see it."

"I always like to see anonymous letters. Get excellent
tips from them. Threw away the best story I ever missed in
New Orleans by not following up one."

Sally was politely interested in a story she had heard
five times, but she handed over the envelope before Andy
got well into the details of that New Orleans fiasco of
twenty years back. It halted the story.

Andy read the sheet of paper, studied it gravely, handed
it to Johnny.

"What did Dick say?" Andy asked.

"Oh, he thought it was just a stunt of one of O'Toole's friends."

"That's all." Rorke pitched the letter back to Andy. "O'Toole's likeable enough, personally. In fact, the bootleggers are getting more and more presentable, as Prohibition goes on, but I think this one's just pulled the wool over your eyes, Sally. I'm inclined to think he killed the woman and the old man; think better of that solution as time goes on. His story is plausible, but he's clever, and he had four days to polish up his alibi."

"Oh, now, Johnny, if you had listened to that story as I did last night, you would believe it, too," Sally protested.

"Tut, tut! O'Toole's nothing but a killer, who was in love with a gal, and her suicide shot him all to pieces, and he just had sense enough left for one thing: to go to the one person who had believed everything Alice had told her. Meaning our Sally. He says Alice was with him in Galveston when the fire broke out. Nobody could prove that alibi but Alice, and now she's dead. And don't forget that Alice didn't say a word about being with O'Toole that night; she told Sally she drove up and down the beach until daylight. We haven't found a soul in Galveston who saw her with O'Toole or without him, during the whole six hours she was away from her room in the hotel."

"Well, I don't know, John. I'm inclined to agree with Sally about O'Toole. Especially since he told me about the Bourbon. Have another, Johnny?" Andy reached behind him and pulled out a drawer of his desk, producing one of the bottles he and Sally had found that morning, and three glasses.

"Sally?"

"No, thanks, Andy. I don't like it much."

"Well, I could care for this brand of Bourbon," Rorke admitted, tossing off his drink. "I reckon I ought to be on O'Toole's side, too. But I'm not, whiskey or no whiskey.

You believe that baby because he has good looks and an Irish tongue. Charming people, the Irish!"

"Let's see that note again, Sally." Andy studied it, turned the page over and over, and then laid it down.

"What does that word 'airplane' down there at the bottom of the page mean?" Sally asked.

"Don't you remember the airplane? The morning of the fire?" Rorke was matter of fact. It flashed back in Sally's memory. The motor roaring just over their heads in the darkness! She clutched Andy's arm.

"Andy! There was! There was a plane flying just over our heads that morning! I hadn't thought of it since!"

Andy, a mocking grin on his face, turned on her.

"Was there? Well, it's a fine reporter you are, young lady! You hear an airplane flying low, right at the scene of a double murder, and you forget it!"

"Andy, I hadn't thought of it since, Things were happening so fast. I'm sorry!"

Sally's humiliation was so apparent that Hunt changed his target at once.

"That's all right, honey," he reassured her, mocking at Rorke now. "Little Johnny was on the job. Not that he found out anything.

"What did you find out about that plane?" Sally asked the infallible Rorke.

"Well—and don't repeat this to any one, darling; it may solve the Blair case—I found out that some of the neighbors had heard a plane fooling around out there twice before, once just before Christmas and once about six weeks before that. Several people heard it each time, and from their descriptions of the noise, I think the bird made a landing on that space, probably on one of the graveled streets. That would be risky, but possible. Everybody who heard the plane, both times, agreed that it didn't stay three minutes before it took off."

"But what would a plane be doing there?" Sally wondered aloud.

"That's exactly what Andy and I have been trying to find out. I haven't had time to follow up on the plane angle, what with this wild goose chase after your Irish cavalier, but I have a hunch that the plane had something to do with that house and the queer doings in it."

"Could he have been bringing in liquor?" Sally hazarded.

"In this town? With seventy-odd steamship lines running up to the back door? It isn't probable. Liquor's too cheap for it to pay any one to carry it here in a plane and risk landing, even if he had landing lights on the plane, on those unlighted streets, so close to Telephone Road that there was a big risk of attracting a flock of cars, even at two o'clock in the morning. And then, how much liquor could they unload out of a plane in three minutes?"

"Never mind worrying about liquor, Johnny," Andy cut in. "I know now what the plane was carrying."

"What?" demanded Sally and Rorke together.

Andy blew a cloud of smoke out the corner of his mouth. "Dope."

It sank in slowly. Rorke, frowning at the toe of one pebbled brown brogue, nodded.

"It could be," he admitted, doubtfully.

"It could be," Andy repeated. "Linking it up to the tipoff in this note, I've got a hard hunch that it was."

"A man could carry twenty—fifty—even a hundred thousand dollars' worth of the stuff in a cabin plane, in two or three suitcases—" Rorke thought aloud.

"And bring it up from Mexico," Andy supplied.

"And dump it out and go back without refueling, if he had auxiliary gas tanks in the ship. There's plenty of commercial jobs that could make it here from Brownsville and back on one load of gas. Um— Risky, but, with the profit on dope what it is, worth the risk to any pilot who didn't care how he made his money."

Andy whirled to his telephone and called the police station. He asked for the chief. The girl at the switchboard said he was not there.

"Where can I get him?"

"Probably at his home, Mr. Hunt. Do you want your police reporter? I think he's in the press room."

"No, I don't want him, and you needn't tell him I called. This is purely personal. I just want to give the chief a drink. Don't say anything. I don't want all those jacka-napes down there to know I have a bottle of good likker. Got just enough for me and the boy friend."

The girl giggled. These newspapermen! You never knew when they were kidding. "You have the chief's home number, haven't you?"

"Oh, yeah, I have that. Much obliged."

Andy called the chief's home.

"Tom? This is Hunt. Say, who's the best dope stool pigeon you got?"

"Why, Andy? What do you want?"

"Get hold of him for me, and find out if old man Fox, this old guy who was burned up, was a dope peddler as well as an addict. And lay low, Tom. Don't breathe this to a soul, and don't let that stool squeak. Get me?"

"Sure, Andy. When do you want this?"

"Everything you can get by to-morrow morning. I'll send Miss Lomax down there for it. Tell her, and nobody else, will you? Much obliged, Tom."

He slammed up the receiver and got out his penknife and a match. The three sat thinking. Finally Andy broke the silence.

"John, do you know any commercial pilots around here?"

"I know Joe Smits. He lives down near Ellington Field. We trained together at Ellington in 'Seventeen."

"Reckon you could catch him at home now?"

"Might."

"Call him up, and then suppose you and Sally drive down in her car and pick him up and take him to San Jacinto Inn for dinner. Pump him for all he knows about any 'mystery planes' around here. Only don't arouse his suspicions; we don't want him telling somebody else."

"Sure. If it's all right with you, Sally?"

That young woman was already on her feet. "Get your overcoat on," she commanded.

"Take this bottle along," the city editor added. "I suppose your friend drinks?"

"Joe? Don't make me laugh." Johnny picked up the telephone book, looked up the number, called it and asked for Smits. He talked in his usual telephone voice, a confidential murmur, exchanging friendly insults with Smits. Presently he put up the receiver and started for the door, the bottle of Bourbon under his arm.

"Wait a minute," Andy called after him. "Got any money?"

Rorke searched his pockets. "Two dollars and a dime. Can you cash a check?"

Andy got out his bill fold and shook his head. "I've got five dollars and some chicken feed."

"Come on, come on," Sally said. "I have two twenty-dollar bills."

"Pipe the idle rich," jeered Rorke, over his shoulder, as he followed her out.

As they got into the roadster, Sally reopened the subject of the airplane.

"Dumb little me, forgetting about that plane!"

"Shucks, you've brought in grand scoops every day, Sally. I've had just one little triumph in this story: that money order receipt."

"Don't be silly! What about the hotel telephone girl?"

"Oh, that!" Rorke changed the subject back to the airplane, the drug traffic, the profits in it.

Smits was waiting for them. They drove through the twilit mist to San Jacinto Battleground, where presently they were attacking oversized oysters while the pleasant odor of frying chicken floated out from the kitchen. The aviator had been fortified on the way down with drafts on the Bourbon bottle; he now had a tall highball beside his plate, looking enough like Sally's glass of ginger ale to pass inspection. The bottle was under the table.

"I'll swear, Johnny," the big fellow rumbled, "that's the best whiskey I've had in years. I've guzzled a pint of that bottle, and I'm no more drunk than Miss Lomax, Prohibitionist that she is!" He grinned gayly at Sally.

"Sorry I can't get any more from that bootlegger, Joe," said Rorke. "If I had your plane, though, I'd never worry about getting good stuff. Say, are there any planes bootlegging from Mexico these days?"

"I hear there's some guy who comes in about once in two months," Smits said. "Always in the dark of the moon. I don't know whether he brings liquor or not."

"Have you ever seen him?" inquired Sally.

"No, but one of the boys at the field did, about Christmas. He's got a cabin monoplane—a Fairchild Wasp job. Four hundred horses on the nose. A fellow could get to Europe in one of those babies."

"That's interesting. Could he bring in much liquor?"

"Well, not enough, Miss Lomax, to make a lot of money at regular bootlegging. I've had a hunch that he works for some guy who can afford to have a dozen cases loaded down on the border, and flown in, so that he can brag to his friends about it."

"More than likely some of these rich Yankee oil men, who want to act smart," said Sally, disgust in her tones.

Both men laughed. Johnny leaned closer to Smits.

"I wonder if he could be bringing in dope. You reckon—?"

"You're cock-eyed! These yarns you guys get up about dope being flown in here give me a pain! Boloney! If that guy was bringing in dope, don't you know one of those Federal dicks would have got him before this? Say, I've got respect left for just two branches of Uncle Sam's family: the postal inspectors and the narcotic men. When those babies don't rap the guilty guy, it's because he's not guilty."

"Johnny, maybe you'd better not have any more of that liquor." Sally put in her word in mock concern.

"I'm sober enough to say 'Around the rugged rock the ragged rascal ran' and that's an official test in this county. You can't blame me for hoping something would come of these stories. They are always too indefinite. I pine to pin one down."

Presently on their way back to Ellington Field, they were singing old army songs with all the fervor of corn liquor harmony.

"It's been a simply grand evening." Sally summed it up as she left Johnny at the door of his apartment in Houston. "That's a good egg, that aviator, and I laughed so much I forgot all about the Blair case."

She drove home, humming "Madelon" as she turned into the driveway and put up her car. Lying on the hall table was something that brought her back to the realm of reality: a Special Delivery letter addressed to Miss Sally Lomax. She tore it open.

"Your right smart but make them give us some
coke, we aint had none since the old man
burned them up and we are all going nuts."

Sally read the note over and over. Upstairs at her dressing table, she put it in her purse. What did it mean? Why should the person who wrote the letter to Dick send one to her? It was in the same handwriting as that of the note Dick had scorned earlier in the day.

She had never come into contact with a drug addict. She had heard, or read, that they were dangerous. Suppose they attacked her or Dick? She tiptoed along the hall to Dick's room; its door was open, the room empty.

Why didn't he come home? For the first time in her sturdy young life, Sally knew what terror was. In panic she began to put on her coat. She would get out of this empty house. But where should she go? She pulled herself up short, breathed deep, relaxed, took off her coat.

Listening for Dick's key, his step on the stairs, she could not settle herself. She took a hot bath, and got into bed. She tried reading, but she couldn't concentrate; so she put the book aside and turned out the light. She counted white sheep going over a wall. They irritated her. Sheep were stupid.

A faint noise at her door! Had the knob been turned? Her heart roared in her ears. She got out of bed, gingerly. The noise came again, faintly. She went to the door.

"Yes?" Timorously.

"Meow?" Scratching!

With a sob of relief, Sally flung open the door and gathered into her arms the great golden Persian cat.

"Abdul Abulbul Emir!" she scolded, hugging the purring beast. "Don't you ever scare me like that again!"

Abdul purred louder, licked her ear. No longer alone, she slid back into bed, the terrors dispelled. A few minutes later she heard Dick's key and his familiar stumble in the hall. Great dumb-bell, he had been stumbling over that lowest step as far back as she could remember! With a sense of safety almost as smug as Abdul's, she snuggled down beside the cat and went to sleep.

11

Arriving at the office next morning, Sally handed her anonymous letter to the city editor without a word. Andy read it, refolded it, replaced it carefully in its envelope. He grunted.

"Fair enough, Sally." He tapped the envelope on his hand. "You run over to the police station and see the chief. Get what he knows about Fox, and then go down and see your friend O'Toole. Don't tell O'Toole anything Tom gives you, but show him these two letters and see what he has to say. When you've done all that, come on in. But remember everything those two tell you."

The chief of police was cordial. "Hello, Miss Sally! I hear you've been doing most of the work on the Blair case. I reckon Dick is jealous, having another member of the family getting famous in his own business. I know I am."

"I don't think so, Chief." Sally closed the door behind her. Her tone discouraged banter. "Mr. Hunt said you had a message to give me for him."

"Sure. He wanted to find out about old man Fox and dope peddling. Well, Andy's a little previous this morning. I haven't been able to get hold of the man I want. I left word last night for him to drop around this morning. Tell Andy if you'll come back about noon to-day, I'll have all the facts."

"May I call Andy from here?"

"Sure. Sure. Use this phone, Miss Sally."

Andy's response was, "Oh, my God! Trust a cop to fool around! All right, kid, run along to the other gent, like I told you, and then come in. You can go back to the station later."

O'Toole appeared to be genuinely glad to see Sally. They shook hands and sat down at the table in the jail corridor.

"This place gives me the same shivers that started me off on pneumonia three years ago, he said. "Have you any news?"

She showed him the two letters. The bootlegger was patently puzzled.

"It's possible the old man did take dope," he said finally, "though I never thought of it before. I just thought he was sort of loony, at times. To tell the truth, Miss Lomax, I never saw the old duffer more than three or four times by daylight. I always went out there at night, and you know how much you can see in lamplight, especially when you are thinking about something else. He always did his job, and that was all that mattered to me."

"What do you think the word 'airplane' means at the bottom of Dick's letter?"

"I haven't the slightest idea."

"Did you ever hear the old man mention an airplane?"

"No."

"Do you think one of your friends could have written those letters?"

"Lord, no! Not without talking to me, first. No, I'd say your letters probably were written by one of the cranks who is always trying to get in on a big crime, like the cranks who confess and know all the while that it can be proved they didn't do the murder. Or else the notes are

honest. If old man Fox was an addict and a peddler, probably more than one of his customers has got the heebie-jee-
bies because he's out of medicine."

Sally smiled. It seemed so far-fetched, this new narcotic angle.

"Sometimes," O'Toole went on, "the way to solve a
mystery is not to be too mysterious about it. Why not
work on the idea that the notes are sincere?"

Sally searched his face for signs of sarcasm. There wasn't
a gleam. It was rather gloomy.

"What's on your program for to-day?"

"Judge Morrison said last night he would be down to
see me sometime during the day. He wants to bring a man
named Potts along for me to talk with; he says Potts will
handle the work on the case for him at present, because he
is swamped. Is Potts any good?"

Sally hesitated at telling O'Toole that the candidate for
governor didn't want to defend a bootlegger. But it had all
worked out just as Andy had predicted. O'Toole did not
notice her hesitation. He went on:

"I'm not so keen about this man Potts. I've heard he's
a hanger-on of Judge Morrison's, but I reckon the best
thing I can do now is let it rock along. If Judge Morrison
don't want to handle the case, himself, I'll get me another
lawyer."

"Oh, yes, there's lots of time before they can bring you
to trial. Mr. O'Toole, do you have any idea where Alice
got that letter in the long blue envelope? Or what she
could have done with it?"

"I was thinking about that last night. What about her
sister's safe deposit box? Some newspaper said she had
been there before she went to see your brother on Friday."

"That's it! That's where she got it!" Sally jumped up.
"I'd forgotten all about that! How dumb of me!"

She took hasty leave of O'Toole and went back to her office, where she told Andy briefly what O'Toole had said, and then asked if she might go down to the bank to see about the Browning safe deposit box.

Colonel Robert Patterson, president of the bank, had known Sally's father and mother; he was right glad to see her. She told him, innocently, that she had come down to ask if he knew anything about the Blair sisters. The old man sighed.

"Did you know them personally, Colonel Bob?"

"Yes, of course I did. I've known Angela Browning ten years. She did her banking, in large part, up here, instead of at Galveston. We have her will; or rather, we have had it since Alice turned it over to me the other day."

"Alice turned it over to you?"

The old gentleman nodded. "Yes, she came in here Friday and went through her sister's deposit box. She had a key and the privilege of using it, though she had never done so. She found the will there, and brought it up to me. Poor girl, I'm glad she did. At least it protects that child—" He stopped abruptly.

"You mean Angela's daughter?" Sally supplied casually.

"You know about that? Angela always tried to keep that to herself; even Alice didn't know about that child until she read the will. It was a great shock to her."

"Do you know what other papers she found in the box?"

"Why, there were a number of bonds, which she left with me, and a letter, which she took off with her."

"Was this the envelope?" Sally took the rumpled blue cover out of her purse.

"Why, yes, it is! Where did you get it?"

Sally told him where and when she had found it. The banker was disturbed.

"She didn't open that letter here," he said. "She said she thought she would go on home before she read it. The poor child! Do you reckon there was something in that

letter that could have made her kill herself? I wish now I
had insisted she read it here at my desk."

"I wish I knew." Sally sighed. "By the way, did Angela
leave much money? What did the will say?"

"Yes, she left a good deal; I'm not prepared to say how
much. The total will depend on what we can do with the
hospital and the shop."

"Did she leave it to Alice or to her daughter?"

"Look here, Sally, you're as cheeky as any other reporter. You want to know too much, young woman!"

Sally leaned over and patted his hand.

"Oh, come on, now, Colonel Bob! Who gets the money?"

"Alice got one-third and the daughter gets two-thirds,
with each one the heir of the other. But Alice's had a
string tied to it, in a codicil. Angela mailed the codicil to
me on Monday night."

Sally's thoughts were racing. So Angela had made a
codicil to her will on Monday!

"This codicil—it was witnessed by a couple of the nurses
in Galveston—stipulated that Alice, if she married this
Terence O'Toole, was not to have anything but a revoking
of the debt due Angela on her shop. Poor little Alice cried
over that, here in my office, Friday."

"Good heavens, Colonel Bob, you can't think she killed
herself over that?"

"I hardly think so; she didn't cry that way, if you know
what I mean. She just sat and sobbed gently and said she
didn't have anything left to live for. I told her she had a
niece to take care of now, and after a while she braced up
and went on home."

"Had the letter that was in this blue envelope been in
the box long?"

"We don't look into the boxes, you know, but I guess
it had. Our records show that Angela hadn't been into her
box for more than two months."

"Well, that letter couldn't have had anything in it about Alice marrying Terry, then, because both Alice and Terry have told me that Angela knew nothing about that until last Monday."

"The day she mailed the codicil cutting off Alice if she should marry O'Toole?"

Sally nodded.

"Well, it's all too much of a muddle for me, Sally."

"We're going to print the story of Angela's daughter to-day, Colonel Bob."

"No, no, you can't do that! What I've told you here is in confidence."

"Yes, but I knew about the child before I came," Sally said sweetly. "When are you going to file the will? And now that Alice is dead, who is going to look after the child?"

"I'm not going to file the will until after the funeral services. The child is a ward of the trust department of the bank. That was arranged some years ago. I have felt, ever since I heard of Angela Browning's death, that she had a premonition something might happen to her."

"I reckon she did. The inscription on this envelope looks that way. But maybe she was just a good business woman; like as not she had read some of your advertisements about protecting the family by making a will and leaving everything to your bank."

"Run along, Sally Lomax. You always were an impudent minx," the colonel growled. "You know too much and you want to know more. Get out!"

Sally laughed and patted the old man's hand.

"Never mind, Colonel Bob; you're my sweetheart and I'm waiting for you to divorce that woman and marry me. You've been promising me you would ever since I was five years old. You be sweet to me, now, or I'll sue you."

She left while the banker was assembling his retort, before he could get back to the topic of what she could and couldn't print.

Andy pushed back his hat as Sally came up to his desk. "Get anything, kid?"

"Lots." Her eyes were blazing. She outlined her story briefly. At least one thing she had learned in the week since the fire in the old house on Telephone Road, a thing she was never to forget while she worked for a newspaper: she could outline a story verbally, briefly, and pointedly. It is a pearl of great price to a city editor, that knack.

"I told Colonel Bob we were going to print the story of the daughter," she finished. "Are we?"

"Certainly! Too bad for the kid, but news is news. Come on; let's get at it. No need to name the kid, or tell exactly where she is in school. Simply say that Angela Browning's daughter is her sole heir. I don't want these other papers to get too much about that: we've got it on ice, and I want to save it for a reason."

"Shall I put in about the lost letter in the blue envelope?"

"Nope. Going to keep that to ourselves a while. I want you to go back out to that apartment as soon as you have finished this story. Go through that place with a fine-tooth comb. Look under the mattress, the bed, and every place she might have stuck that letter. See if you can find a scrap of it. She may have torn it up, and let a piece of it fall."

"Regular Sherlock Holmes stuff, Andy. Must I take a magnifying glass?"

"I reckon your eyes are good enough. Now hit that machine, kid."

As Sally handed in the last of her story on the will, she reminded Andy of the report the chief of police was to give her.

"Light out and get that first, then. Don't telephone me about it; come in."

The police chief closed his office door behind Sally.

"I don't know what Andy is after in this case, Miss Sally," he said. "But it looks to me like he has stumbled on something."

"What?"

"Old man Fox was a dope peddler, all right, a high-priced wholesaler, with the best retailers for clients. No talcum powder in his snow. It was uncut, just like the best bootleggers tell you their rye is. He got his stuff in regularly about once every two months. My—er—informant swears he didn't know of it, himself. Says he got hold of a man last night who was about nutty because he didn't have any, and hadn't had any for several days. He ranted for an hour against you and your brother, my man said. When I went after my stool last night he was out hunting up some heroin for this guy."

Sally whistled.

"How did Andy get on to this?" the chief wanted to know.

"I can't tell you, Chief. Mr. Hunt just asked me to come over here and get a confidential report from you."

"Andy's smart. Well, tell him I'll produce this addict if he wants to talk to him. But he's got to protect my man, you know. His life wouldn't be worth two cents if it got out he was a stool."

"Does this man have any idea where Fox got his drugs?"

"Says he doesn't, and says the happy duster he fixed up last night doesn't, either. All he knows is that Fox got in a big supply every so often."

"Did Fox make his deliveries or did they come out to the house for it?"

"Fox delivered. I told you he had high-class trade. No dollar coke sniffers on his list, the man said."

"Do you think an addict could have set fire to the house on Telephone Road?"

"The case is in your brother's hands, Miss Sally. I can't make any such predictions when they have O'Toole under arrest, without 'damaging the state's case,' as they say."

"Oh, bosh!" remarked the district attorney's sister. "Well, anyway, thanks a lot, Chief. Mr. Hunt said you'd keep this to yourself?"

"Sure. Forget it. It's a county case. If they want facts, they can get what I've got by asking. But I'm not putting out." The amiable, big police chief grinned.

Sally's report to Andy was not used in the home edition. She wondered why. Andy had merely nodded when she recounted it, carefully. He went on whittling at a match, and she stood waiting at the corner of his desk.

"Oh, Havens!" Andy bawled across the city room. "I want you to go out with Miss Lomax on a story," he instructed when the reporter had come to his desk. "She'll tell you what to do."

He turned to his newly created star.

"Havens can help you look that apartment over. If you find what we want, I'll buy you a box of cigars."

"Cigars?"

Andy came out of his detachment and grinned.

"All great detectives smoke cigars. Before you go, lend me a cigarette. There's not a clew in a carload."

12

They looked in every book, on every shelf, in every drawer, under the rugs, behind the pictures, in all the pockets of the smart and dainty garments that had been Alice Blair's, under and behind everything movable from living-room to kitchen cabinet. When they had finished after two hours of inch by inch progress, Sally and Havens were able to tell the city editor that not a scrap of the missing letter was in the Blair apartment. The *Pioneer's* own Scotland Yard was baffled.

"It's gone, entirely," Sally told Andy Hunt over the telephone. "Havens even went out back and searched through the trash cans in the court. But the janitor said she hadn't set out any trash Friday night, and no garbage Thursday night except coffee grounds. There were a lot of coffee grounds in the garbage pail where Manning found the whiskey bottle; we even turned those out on a newspaper. And, Andy—in the coffee grounds there was the butt of a cigar. It struck us as sort of funny. You see, she had set out the garbage pail Thursday night and got it back empty Friday morning, so these must be Friday's coffee grounds. Havens says it's a small pantela shape and very good tobacco; he's got it wrapped up and we'll bring it in."

"Good stuff," commended Andy. "You don't think she smoked a cigar before she shot herself, to steady her nerves, maybe?"

"Andy! Don't be too horrid! Havens and I think it's a clew."

"So do I." Andy was serious again. "The two of you keep it strictly to yourselves. Well, come on in and stick around. Tell Havens I'd like for him to relieve Carter at your brother's office. Nothing particular. Just watch for anything to turn up."

Sally left Havens at the Fannin Street steps of the courthouse and drove on to the office. It was then half-past four. Drake, the assistant city editor, Andy and the sporting editor were the only men in the city room.

She picked up the *Pioneer* and the *Record* final editions from Andy's table and went over to her desk. A two-column head on the front page of the *Pioneer,* below the fold, caught her eye:

AIRMAN, LOST IN FOG, CRASHES INTO BARN

Special to *The Pioneer*

Alvin, Tex., Feb. 20.—Losing his way in the fog and coming down to try to get his bearings, Steve Daly, airman, crashed into the silo at the end of the dairy barn of J. R. Jeffries, four miles east of here on the Galveston Road, at two o'clock this morning. The right wing was torn off his machine, a Fairchild cabin monoplane, and it fell into the soft mud of the barnyard.

Daly was bruised and cut about the face and was unconscious when Jeffries, hearing the crash, ran out and picked him up. The dairyman rushed the pilot to Alvin by automobile. His injuries were dressed by Dr. F. R. Winn. He had come to on the ride into town.

Jeffries said the aviator told him he was flying from Tampico to Dallas to buy another plane when he lost his bearings in the fog.

Beyond saying that the pilot was not seriously injured, Dr. Winn would not comment on a report that Daly had been taken to Houston by a local county officer before daylight.

The *Record* had practically the same story.

Sally went over to the city desk, carrying the papers. Andy looked up from his work and spiked another sheet on the spindle.

"Andy, don't you think this airplane is worth looking into? It's the same make of plane as the one Joe Smits told us about."

Hunt grinned.

"You'll be city editor yet, kid. Where do you think Johnny Rorke has been all day? Not hanging around your distinguished brother's doorstep."

"But why did you get this story so late?"

"It was in the home edition; our Alvin man phoned it in before noon, which was none too speedy of him at that." Andy picked a home edition off the table and handed it to her.

"Well, I just overlooked it," said Sally. "What did Johnny find out?"

"Now, listen, kid: I haven't got time to gossip right now. But I've got a date at your brother's office at five o'clock and you can go along if you want to and won't ask any questions of anybody. Here, take this copy out to Dad, will you?" He pulled the papers off the copy spindle.

The foreman of the composing room was at his desk, making out time reports with a stub of a pencil. Besides the regular night operators, already busy at some of the linotype machines, there were two day make-up men idling about who should have been dressed and gone ere this, for the presses had already run the night edition, and halted.

"What's the old man got now, Miss Sally?" asked a printer as she started back.

"I don't know; why?"

"Is he going extra?"

"Not that I know of; why?"

"Held the day crew on here and downstairs."

"Well, I don't know a thing about it. How long are you to stay?"

The man shrugged. "Until he tells us to go."

Sally trudged beside Andy on the way to the courthouse, eager to know why the crew was being held, but aware, from Andy's face, that it was wiser to keep silence. It was threatening rain and growing cold.

They had reached the steps of the courthouse when a newsboy came racing down the street yelling "Extry! Extry!"

Andy's face turned brick red. He snatched a paper from the boy, leaving Sally to get one for herself and pay for both. She gasped as she read:

MYSTERY HOUSE BURNED DOWN!

The *Record* had gone extra with the story that the old house on Telephone Road, where Angela Blair Browning and Martin Fox, poisoned and partly cremated, had met death, had caught fire again at four-thirty that afternoon and, fanned by the high north wind, had burned to the ground before the fire department could stop it. No clew as to the cause of the second fire had been found.

Sally waited for Andy's explosion.

"Nice story," he said amiably, starting up the steps. "Yeah, nice enough. Our man at the fire station phoned me half an hour ago that he was going out on a fire somewhere on the edge of town. I don't know why he didn't phone this in before I left the office. But Drake will get it."

"Aren't—aren't you going to put out a paper on it, Andy?" Sally asked meekly.

"Nope. Let 'em have one story all their own. They need it."

Sally swallowed. It was unbelievable! Andy scooped, and serene! Incredible! Rorke, when she told him this, would call her a liar.

"Where is Johnny?" she demanded, suddenly, as they entered the murky hall of justice and taxes.

"Supposed to meet us here."

They approached the foot of the grandiose marble staircase in the rotunda, turned to the right, and ascended in the elevator to the third floor. In the anteroom of Dick Lomax's offices they found Havens playing penny ante with George Monroe and Roscoe Eddy.

"Good evening, Mr. Hunt," chorused the men from the rival papers. If Monroe saw the *Record* extras in Andy's and Sally's hands, he was elaborately unaware of them.

"Nice scoop, Monroe," said the *Pioneer's* city editor, handing over his copy. "Dick send for you two?"

The three men looked up from their eager scanning of the extras. Eddy nodded.

At that minute Terence O'Toole came in, handcuffed to a deputy sheriff. Released, he shook hands with Sally and then with Hunt. The city editor drew him off into a corner to talk in low tones, Hunt doing most of it, the prisoner answering briefly. As Andy turned from O'Toole, with a hearty slap on the man's shoulder, Bob Morrison came in.

"Hello! Hello, folks! Well, Andy, I see you've got my client in a better mood. Miss Sally! How's the clever girl reporter to-day? Dick will have to look to his laurels. Andy, I hope you've given this girl a raise? She's the best man on your staff."

"I'll give her another and send you the bill if you don't stop putting big ideas in little girls' heads," Andy growled. "Where's Potts? Isn't he coming to this tea party?"

"Henry telephoned me that he would be delayed, but he'll be here."

"Did you see the *Record* extra, Bob?" Andy went on. "Somebody saved you the trouble of tearing down your wreckage."

"Yes, I saw the paper. There seems to be a jinx on that place."

The door of Lomax's private office opened, and a stenographer came down the passageway to look into the anteroom.

"Mr. Lomax would like to see you, Judge Morrison. Bring O'Toole in with you."

There was a tedious wait of ten minutes. George Monroe fidgeted at a window; Sally sat very quiet at a table, penciling rows of interlaced S's on a sheet of copy paper; Andy read the *Record* extra as though it were amusing, instructive, and quite new to him; Havens and Eddy dealt poker hands, bet mildly, shuffled the greasy cards. The deputy, seated in a corner, perused the extra.

The door of the district attorney's office was opened again. Lomax came out.

"Good evening," he said, looking around. "Will you folks come into my office?"

The six trooped in through the passageway, and there was a polite shuffle to offer the district attorney's sister a chair, which embarrassed her. Then they were seated, waiting, eyeing each other.

"O'Toole wants to talk to you newspapermen," said Lomax. "He feels that there is a good deal that you should know; part of it some of you already know, he says. Judge Morrison believes he is making a mistake," here the district attorney threw his friend a smile, "but he consents, since his client so earnestly wishes it."

O'Toole appeared at ease. Much of the acute weariness that Sally had seen in his face on Saturday afternoon had gone, although there were still heavy lines in it, and the eyes still burned in dark caverns.

The district attorney's stenographer, tiptoeing in, seated himself across the table from O'Toole.

"You understand, O'Toole, that this statement you are making in my presence," the district attorney warned, "may be used against you in court?"

O'Toole nodded impatiently.

"I understand that, Mr. Lomax, but I am not under indictment, and if there is any justice in the world, I never will be, so I have no reason for not talking. I intend to tell nothing but the truth, so far as I know it, and the truth can't hurt me."

The telephone rang. With a word of apology the district attorney picked up one of the instruments on his desk.

"This is Lomax."

Sally was at her brother's left after he had turned in his revolving chair to answer the telephone, which was sitting on the desk slide almost against her arm. She had chosen this chair, a little in the background, out of a desire not to appear too conspicuously at home in her brother's office; she had already embarrassed him enough by her *Pioneer* connection. It now appeared that her "rabbit's foot" had followed her even here. The man talking to Dick had one of the vibrant, metallic voices that make a telephone receiver fairly clang; one of those who invariably talk too loud over the wire. The district attorney unconsciously pulled the receiver a little away from his ear, so that he would not be deafened by the brazen voice. And Sally, her left ear not six inches from the receiver, could hear him perhaps a bit more clearly than her brother could.

"Say, this is Hicks at the Federal Building. I've got a prisoner here that wants to talk to you."

"Sorry. I'm busy right now. Who is he?"

"An aviator. He crashed into a silo near Alvin in the fog early this morning."

"Into what?"

"Into a silo on a dairy barn. Busted his machine to glory, but he ain't hurt bad. The town marshal took him over and brought him up to me. He had a satchel of drugs in his plane, worth about twenty thousand dollars, maybe. Biggest haul this year. He was bringin' them in from Mexico."

"Well, congratulations, but where do I come in? That's a Federal case."

"Why, this feller knows something important about the murders in that old house that was set afire—the Browning woman and the old man. He wants to talk to you."

Sally saw Dick's face go tense. He kept his voice carefully casual.

"Well, I've got a conference on now, but I'll be through in maybe half an hour. Why don't you and your friend come on over and wait for me? Just go into Mr. Morton's office; he's gone for the day. And I'll be with you as soon as I get through with these gentlemen. Right."

He hung up and turned to face the table again.

"A fellow wants me to use my influence with Judge Henderson, as if anybody had any." He laughed. "He doesn't know the Judge." It shocked Sally, catching her brother in such a barefaced lie; he was always so brutally honest at home. Well, that was the way the game was played. She had been a sneak and an eavesdropper and felt proud of herself.

"Sorry to have kept you waiting," Dick went on. "Go ahead, O'Toole."

O'Toole plunged into the middle of his story.

"I brought Angela Browning from Galveston to Houston on the evening before she was poisoned and burned. She was my partner in my business. She had loaned me the money to start off with and she had kept on backing me and taking half the profits. I came up here to make arrangements for the delivery of a load of booze that was due in on a freighter Saturday night. We kept our supplies in a cellar we had dug under that old house on Telephone Road. Old man Fox was the caretaker of the house. If you want to prosecute me for bootlegging"—he looked at the district attorney—"go ahead. I'll tell the truth and take the consequences later."

Sally saw Eddy and Monroe look at each other. Eddy looked at the office door, started to rise in his chair, subsided.

The district attorney said nothing. Judge Morrison cleared his throat. His face was beet red.

"You should make no statements here that you haven't already discussed with me," he addressed O'Toole sharply. He looked around the room. "You will pardon my interruption, gentlemen, but this man is confessing to things that he hadn't confided even to his lawyer. I may say that I took this case at the solicitation of Mr. Hunt, whose paper I represent as attorney, but I did not anticipate being made a fool of in this way. I really don't feel—"

"That's all right, Judge Morrison," O'Toole put in hastily. "Mr. Hunt and Miss Lomax heard that part of the story on Saturday night before they turned me over to the state authorities. I just supposed they had passed it on to you. You will recollect that I told you everything but the part about Mrs. Browning's being my partner in the business. I just thought I wouldn't bring that up any more; it looks like I was trying to blacken the name of a dead woman who was mighty kind to me. But when I started to talk just now, you gentlemen were sitting there so plainly expecting me to give you a cock and bull story—it was written all over your faces —that I got sore in spite of myself and started spilling the beans."

"Let the boy alone, Bob," Hunt cut in. "If he tells only what he told me Saturday night, he won't be hanging himself."

O'Toole went on more calmly, a little awkward when he came to telling of his love affair with Alice, of his plan to be married and go to California, but doggedly determined, it seemed to Sally, to withhold nothing. He told of Angela's bitter attack upon him on the ride up from Galveston, of her dull fury after she began drinking with old Fox at the old house, of her rising temper as she drank more.

"She was pretty nasty by the time she ordered me to get out. Old man Fox was as drunk as a Lord."

"Why did she order you to leave?" Eddy wanted to know.

"She was expecting a visitor to meet her out there. The old man told her: 'You ought to know he won't come in while they's a car parked outside.'"

"You have no idea who this visitor was?"

"No, I have not. If I knew who he was, I'd know enough to solve this thing. I believe that person poisoned Mrs. Browning and the old man, and set the house afire, and had the blood of a third innocent person on his hands when Alice Blair . . . shot herself."

"Alice Blair didn't shoot herself, Terry."

Andy Hunt's voice was uncommonly gentle. He was seated in the background by the door, his chair tilted against the wall, whittling at a match stick. Every person in the room whirled around or looked up to stare at him. The traditional pin would have crashed to the floor in the silence.

"What did you say?" The district attorney's words were bullet-like.

"I said Alice Blair didn't shoot herself. She was murdered, more coldly than her sister and Martin Fox. Somebody visited Alice Blair on Friday night, with enough morphine in whiskey to kill three women, got it down her, laid her out on her bed, unconscious, and shot her through the mouth to make it look like suicide."

There was another stupefied silence.

"The *Pioneer* had a private autopsy performed and a chemical analysis made of her stomach. The person who killed Angela and the old man also killed Alice."

The clanging silence that followed this even-voiced judgment was broken by a rap at the door. Hunt leaped to his feet and opened it.

A tall thin man, the image of the old-fashioned barrister, with black hair and a skin as white as Morrison's, stood in the doorway, an apologetic smile on his long, thin face.

"I trust you gentlemen will forgive my being late. I had to go out to the country to see a bedridden client who wanted to make her will."

Lomax arose and shook hands with the newcomer across the table.

"All of you gentlemen know Mr. Potts, I believe. And this is my sister, Sally."

Sally took the lean hand he offered. It was cold as ice.

13

The group in the district attorney's room was just settling down, Potts in a chair brought in from the next office, when the door swung open. Two men stood there, looking in at the startled eleven.

The shorter of the intruders was bedecked with adhesive tape and surgical gauze, hiding half his face. All but O'Toole and Sally recognized the other as Clem Hicks, Federal narcotic inspector.

"Just wait in the office to your right there, will you, Mr. Hicks?" The district attorney did not hide his annoyance.

"Excuse me, Mr. Lomax. I didn't recall which office was which."

Hicks backed out, closing the door. The click of the latch released a jumble of questions, expostulations, demands for Andy Hunt to explain his conclusion.

A sharp rap at the door cut in. Sally saw her brother bite his lower lip, controlling his temper with an effort.

"Excuse me just a few minutes," he said, loud enough to be heard through the crossfire of questions being shot at Hunt. He hurried out, closing the door sharply.

O'Toole's lawyer spoke up hastily, authoritatively. "I think you'd better stop your story here, then, O'Toole, until I have discussed this with you in private."

"Private, hell!" Monroe was aroused. "This case is busted wide open, Judge. We're all in on this. Come on, Mr. Hunt, tell us how much of this hooey is authentic? Why haven't you printed it?"

"Calm down, George, calm down!" Andy was unperturbed. "I've kept it out because I haven't known it but a couple of hours and I had a good reason for not printing it. I think we are on the trail of the man who did the killing."

"What's back of it? Dope?"

"You're a good reporter, Roscoe, but you didn't guess fast enough on that one."

Monroe got up and started toward the door. Andy caught his sleeve as he passed.

"Here, George! Wait awhile. Remember, this is more or less a *Pioneer* party. You're not privileged to use our news until we release it."

"The hell I'm not!"

"Mr. Hunt's right," said Eddy, suavely.

"Sure, you'll say that. You've got a nine o'clock edition coming. My crew will be gone in another fifteen minutes." Monroe's face was a brick red. He moved a step toward the door. Andy rose, calmly, and stood with his back against the closed door. His voice changed not a perceptible tone.

"That's right, George. Well, call your office over this phone and tell them to hold the crew for you. Unless I'm mistaken, there will be plenty of news for everybody within the next couple of hours." Sally pushed Lomax's private phone towards Monroe.

"Already got it in type, Mr. Hunt?" Eddy grinned at Hunt, who grinned back, while they listened closely to what Monroe was saying to his office. Neither of them noticed Lomax open the door and beckon Judge Morrison into the passage. The door closed softly behind the lawyer. As Monroe turned from the phone, Andy spoke again.

"Now, let's settle down and wait for the rest of this yarn. It's not finished yet."

He lighted a cigarette and passed the packet around. There was a tension in the room, the more real for everyone's ignoring it so pointedly. Eddy drummed a dead march on the table with deliberate fingers; Sally scribbled patterns in pencil on a memorandum pad on her brother's desk. Havens, back to the room, hands in pockets, watched the wind whirling newspapers and rubbish across the back lawn of the courthouse square below. Raindrops were streaking the window. Hunt, his chair teetered back against the wall again, studied the lighted end of his cigarette as a rare and precious stone, turning the paper tube between his fingers. O'Toole, his face a gray mask in the failing light, chewed at a cigar, unlighted.

The tableaux of nonchalance was shattered by three sudden sounds: a thud that shook the floor of the office; the slamming of a door that shook open the door at Andy's left, creaking as it swung sharply in; a scream.

The scream, one sharp explosion of mortal terror, brought them up standing. The door at the end of the passage was wrenched open. As one man, those nearest the door made for it. O'Toole and Sally rose last, looking at each other.

Andy Hunt led the scramble through the door and along the empty passage. Sally, on the heels of the last man, heard the clatter of running feet outside in the rotunda, slapping the bare marble, as she peered around the door into the corridor that ran along the well of the rotunda under the courthouse dome. She could hear men racing down the stairs. Havens, Monroe and Eddy, their backs to her, were leaning over the iron railing gazing down into the rotunda well. As one man, they broke for the stairway going down. Lomax's stenographer was standing at the elevator shaft, shouting down it, his thumb on the bell button.

Sally, moving swiftly to the balustrade, looked down and flung up her hands to cover her eyes. Terence O'Toole, coming belatedly out of the office door, caught her as she staggered back from the railing. His left arm around her, he edged over to look down.

On the marble floor at the foot of the grand staircase lay something not pleasant to see. It was, or had been, Judge Robert E. Lee Morrison, attorney, real estate operator, prospective candidate for governor of the state.

14

When Sally, steadying herself, peered again down the dark rotunda well, a knot of people had gathered around the sprawled body: elevator men, porters, scrub-women, a few clerks, the bald-headed deputy tax collector, the blind cigar stand owner, the two men who had blundered into the district attorney's office, the three newspaper reporters, Andy Hunt, hatless for once. Her brother was kneeling beside the body, fumbling at the heart, feeling the wrists. Johnny—where had he come from? The clamor of voices echoed and re-echoed up the well to the dome and back in a staccato jumble. O'Toole's clenched hand was hurting her left arm. Instinctively she tried to pull away. O'Toole held on.

"Don't go down there, Miss Sally," he advised in a flat voice. "You couldn't do a thing to help."

She was willing enough not to, so she gripped the balustrade fearfully and hung over, watching, with sick fascination, the men roll over the body onto its back, lift the head onto someone's rolled-up raincoat. A policeman shouldered in, talked to Dick, who stood up. Men came hurrying into the scene from the street; the policeman suddenly became assertive with a bellow of "Get back! Get back, there!" Like a scene in a movie, so real it seemed, and so remote.

An ambulance gong clattered faintly. The crowd divided. Two men and a stretcher. She looked away, moving uncertainly into the district attorney's office corridor where she knew there was a water cooler. Her throat was parched, her lips dry. O'Toole followed her and stood by, silent, as she gulped. He drank heartily after her, wiping his lips with the back of his hand, deep in thought. Sally was trying to put the tragic picture puzzle together; until that moment she had been merely seeing, registering, studying it in a sort of state of suspended animation.

"What happened?"

O'Toole shrugged.

They heard the click and rattle of the elevator gate down the hall and whirled about. Through the door came Hicks, the bandaged man, the deputy sheriff who had brought O'Toole from jail, the district attorney. Of all the faces, her brother's was the whitest; he and the bandaged man alone appeared to be shaken by what had just happened. The man with the bandages was holding his hand to his jaw; he seemed to be in pain.

Sally and O'Toole followed close on the heels of the four, along the passage into the district attorney's private office.

"What happened?" Sally demanded again.

Her brother's voice seemed to have lost all its resonance, all its biting edge.

"This is Mr. Hicks, the Federal narcotic inspector, and this man," indicating the slight young man with the bandages leaning against the table, "is Mr. Daly—I didn't get your first name—"

"Steve," put in Hicks.

"Steve Daly, an airplane pilot, who has just solved the Blair case for us." Dick was recovering his poise; his sense of the dramatic was coming back to life.

O'Toole and Sally spoke together.

"How?"

Dick Lomax sat down in his swivel chair, pressed his hands over his eyes, sighed. Then he answered, patiently.

"Daly is a commercial aviator, flying out of Tampico. He crashed this morning at Alvin and was picked up senseless but not much hurt." The aviator managed a crooked grin.

"He was turned over by the authorities down there to Mr. Hicks, because there was a suitcase in his plane that had about twenty thousand dollars' worth of narcotic drugs in it. He insisted that he should come over here and tell me what he knew of the fire in the old house on Telephone Road. Mr. Hicks called me up while O'Toole was talking in here, and I told him to bring Daly on over and wait in the other office. They blundered in here."

"Well, we didn't exactly do that," Hicks put in apologetically. "It was Johnny Rorke's idea that we should bust in here like that so Daly could get a look at the crowd. Rorke had told him he'd likely find the guilty man sitting in this office."

The district attorney turned beet red.

"Where is Rorke?" he snapped, looking around.

"I seen him get into the ambulance with Judge Morrison," the deputy sheriff volunteered.

O'Toole had been leaning across a chair back, his hands gripping its arms. He cleared his throat huskily.

"Well, for God's sake, what happened out there?" he said in a shaking voice.

Lomax turned, slowly.

"Daly saw us sitting at the table here and thought we had already arrested the murderer of old man Fox and Angela Browning, just as Rorke had said we would have. Daly told Hicks so."

"He said he reckoned he was too late to help you much," broke in Hicks. "I asked him what he meant and he said you had the right man, all right. I asked him which one, and he said the tall black-haired fellow at the end of the table was the one. 'Why,' I says, 'that's Judge Morrison. That ain't no murderer.' But he stuck to it, and described the man and it was Morrison he meant, sure enough. I was bumfuzzled and I went and broke in on you all again and called Mr. Lomax out. And Mr. Lomax didn't believe what Daly said no more than I did. So he called Judge Morrison out, and you know what happened."

"What?" It was O'Toole, his eyes blazing.

The aviator came to life suddenly. His voice startled Sally when he spoke; it was clipped, almost cockney English.

"I said to Mr. Lomax, as I had said to this gentleman, that this Judge Morrison, as they called the fellow, was the man I had seen in old Fox's house, pouring oil over everything and then setting it afire. And Mr. Lomax called this fellow out, and made me repeat it to his face. And the next thing we knew, he had swung on my jaw, and I was knocked across the desk, and he was out of the room in one jump and slammed the door behind him. And then he jumped off the balcony."

"I think he fell over the railing," Lomax interposed. "I think he must have come out of the door too fast and skidded on the floor. You all remember it was wet; the scrubwoman was just mopping up." He paused for corroboration. Now that Dick spoke of it, Sally recalled that she had noticed the floor was wet and slippery, but the fact hadn't registered.

"Well," said Hicks, slowly, "that's a good way to explain it, but I think he jumped. Of course, nobody saw him, and you may be right."

O'Toole cut in, addressing the aviator.

"You say you saw Morrison set the house afire. Where were you?"

"I was outside looking through the crack at the side of the window shade, into the front room. I could see the old man lying on the divan back against the staircase, asleep or drunk. Then this fellow Morrison came out of the next room, with a five gallon can of petrol, I thought it must be, but I knew they burned oil lamps—there was one on the table there, as a matter of fact—so I decided it must be paraffin, or kerosene, as you call it up here. He was pouring the last of the stuff onto the carpet, and then he remembered the old fellow on the divan and poured what was left on his clothes. I don't mind admitting I got the wind up. While I was trying to decide what to do with a dangerous maniac, I saw him light a match and set a newspaper afire and toss it right toward me. There was a flare-up, and an explosion and I jumped back off the veranda, and ran for my plane and went away from there as fast as I could jump her off the ground. You see," he grinned ruefully, "I had the same parcel of—er—imported goods that I had this morning when I cracked up in your charming village of Alvin, and I really can't be blamed for clearing out . . ."

"Then it was your plane we heard cross the road just as we got to the fire?" Sally blurted.

"You heard? Who heard?" Her brother whirled on her.

"Johnny Rorke and I heard a plane, flying low, but the fire drove it right out of my mind until Sunday when you got that anonymous letter with 'airplane' at the bottom of it. Mr. Hunt and Mr. Rorke have been working on that clew ever since. It was really they who solved the murders."

"What's this?" asked Daly sharply.

"We'll discuss that later," the district attorney said. "I'd like to ask you a few questions, unofficially. You don't have to answer if you don't wish to. You're taking a plea of guilty, I presume?"

The aviator shrugged. "What else can I do? This chap's been after me for months and he knows more about my affairs than I do."

"He'll plead guilty if he knows what's good for him," said Hicks tartly. "And I think he does."

"Do I understand you carried narcotics to old man Fox?"

"He did," commented Hicks dryly. "At least three trips that we know of. They were pretty slick, though. We know a big supply was coming in about every two months, but we thought it came off a boat in the Ship Channel. Then we got wind of this airplane business."

"How?" asked Daly casually.

"Wouldn't you like to know?" Hicks grinned. "This old man Fox was the wholesaler, but I'm satisfied he was just working for someone higher up; he couldn't have thought up this plan and carried it out; didn't have the brains; didn't have the capital. Why, they even had that fake real estate subdivision laid out there with two graveled streets, extra wide, crossing so they made a landing field for this fellow's plane, no matter which way the wind was blowing. That took thinking and money."

"Wait a minute," said O'Toole, who had relaxed into a chair, but who now sat up straight. "That property belonged to Judge Morrison, didn't it?"

"Yes, it did," the district attorney admitted, rather reluctantly. Even yet he hadn't grasped all of the ramifications in which his friend appeared to have dealt. This affair was more of a hazy dream than reality to Richard Lomax.

"Then he must have been the man higher up in this dope ring, or in cahoots with them. It don't stand to reason he wasn't."

"No, it don't, does it?" Hicks agreed, scratching his neck.

"What sort of a plane did you have?" Lomax turned again to the aviator.

"A Fairchild Wasp job—a cabin monoplane, you know, with an extra gas tank in the fuselage, that I had put in. That gives it a fifteen-hundred-mile cruising radius; I could fly here from Tampico and back without refueling, and get up here from Tampico and back again between dark and daylight. I never stayed three minutes at this end. A fellow they called Canfield would always meet me when I landed, pay me in gold, check the stuff sitting in the cabin with the curtains down—I had curtains put on her—and beat it to the house and I'd be right off. . . . She was a good old bus, but she's gone now." He turned to Hicks.

"I say, could I get somebody to take the motor out of her and keep it for me?"

"I reckon that can be fixed. The plane's in the hands of the government now, and pretty safe. And so are you."

"Why did you come back if you knew about the fire and the murders?" Sally asked suddenly.

"Well, I didn't know about the woman; I never did see her. I sent a wire from Tampico to the man we called Tom Canfield here in Houston. I got the answer night before last in Tampico. I had wired him I had gone back, as landing was unsafe. We used a code that read like a harmless message. He wired back to come ahead, and I did. I supposed maybe the old man had waked up and got out and the house either burned down or didn't; I didn't know. I hadn't seen any of your newspapers, of course. But I had ten thousand pesos' worth of stuff, at Tampico prices, to deliver before I'd get paid, and I decided to take a chance. There was a norther predicted on the way, but I figured I'd beat it here and back. Then I ran into this damned fog, and got lost and came down trying to get my bearings and hit this—what do you call it? Silo? A rum end, if you ask me."

The door opened unceremoniously and in walked Andy Hunt, followed by Henry Potts and a policeman. Both Hunt and Potts were disheveled; there was a bleeding scratch on Hunt's right cheek.

Hunt addressed the district attorney.

"This man," indicating Potts with a jerk of his head, "had left the courthouse practically on the run. I overtook him and tried to bring him back and he resisted. The officer here interfered, and I got him to bring us up here to settle it. This man Potts is a material witness in this case and he was on his way elsewhere when I grabbed him. If you want a charge to hold him on, I'll charge him with being the head of a drug ring, or with arson for burning down that house this afternoon, or having it set afire; I'll charge him with anything, just so you hold him for me."

"Explain yourself, Hunt," the bewildered district attorney demanded. Potts had collapsed into the chair at the end of the table—the chair Morrison had sat in earlier.

"All right. I'll ask Potts to answer me this. Were you in the drug business with Martin Fox? Yes or no? I can prove you are a morphine addict."

"I'll make no statement," said Potts weakly, "until I have been properly arrested and accused. I have a right to an examination before a justice of the peace."

The little aviator, sitting in the shadow at the far end of the roll-top desk, leaned forward.

"I think the game's up, Mr. Canfield. If I were you, I'd make a clean breast of it. They've got me dead to rights, and I mean to plead guilty and take my medicine."

Potts started up out of the chair, but the huge policeman, moving catlike across the room, caught him by the shoulders from behind and forced him down again.

"Take it easy, partner," he advised.

Hunt, facing Potts down the length of the table, shot another bolt.

"If you try to fight this, you'll end up by being tried for murder. Were you with Morrison when he poisoned those two and set the house afire?"

"I was not," said Potts wearily. "I was waiting out on the field, with a flashlight, to signal that bastard over there. Morrison went in the house alone. That hell cat of a wife of his, Angela, had found out about the drug business and called him out there. They had a hell of a quarrel; I could hear her yelling at him clear out on the field. This fellow was later than usual. After a while the racket died down. I went back to the house for a minute, and there were the woman and the old man, laid out cold and Morrison with an oil can and a lot of newspapers. I took one look and ran. I got in my car and left him. I reckon he walked back to town, after he started the fire."

"All right," said Hunt. "That's clear. Now, who killed Alice Blair? Did you?"

Sally cast a fearful glance at O'Toole as he moved. The man seemed waiting, ready to spring. "It wouldn't take long to fill a skunk full of lead," the girl could hear those passionate words echoing again. But no, O'Toole couldn't have a gun now! She looked over at Potts, struggling for words; the man was broken.

"Before God, no, gentleman. I wouldn't kill a fly." Tears were rolling down the man's cheeks as he stared helplessly at the irate little person at the other end of the table. He turned to appeal to the district attorney.

"All I did was to get the whiskey for him. This Alice Blair called him up at the club at nine o'clock last Friday night. He got me out of bed and told me to come over there and bring him two pints of the good Bourbon that O'Toole there 'provides for his friends.' I was sick, too."

"Wait a minute." O'Toole's voice had something deadly in it. "You can't drag me into this."

"Sit down." Potts' smile was macabre. "All you are is a simple-minded, hard-working and honest bootlegger." He turned to Lomax again. "He didn't know anything about the drug racket. We didn't trust him that far. We started it only last fall as a side line to the bootlegging. I'll take credit for thinking up this airplane business."

"Well, what happened after you got to Morrison's apartment?" Hunt demanded.

"He told me that Alice Blair, his wife's sister, had got a letter out of Angela's safe deposit box telling all about their marriage—their shotgun wedding"—Potts smiled nastily—"the little girl up in Virginia—"

"Had you known about that before?" Lomax cut in.

"I knew them both up in Dallas fifteen years ago. You might say Morrison had no secrets from me."

"You might say that's how you've made a living these past ten years," commented Hunt. "Just knowing things about Morrison. Did you make an addict out of him?"

"Well, not exactly. He broke his leg, you may recollect, a year ago in that automobile wreck when the truck hit him on the Galveston Road. He came out of the hospital sooner than he should, and the leg gave him hell, and he wanted something to ease the pain, so I gave him morphine, and that's the way he got the habit."

Lomax was shaking his head sadly. "What a pity—what a pity! A man like Bob Morrison!"

"Whited sepulchers," Hunt shot at him, grimly. "You ought to be a newspaperman, Lomax. You'd never be surprised at anything. I've known drug addicts in higher places than Morrison's. What happened next about Alice Blair?"

"Why, he asked me for a tube of morphine sulphate, and I gave him a full five grains—in quarter grain tablets, you know. He took that and the whiskey and went out to see her. He had no trouble at all getting past your men at that hour." Potts smiled sardonically at the district attorney. "They were just looking for O'Toole. And he got out the back way, quite easily, about midnight. I was waiting for him at his place. He was as drunk as a fool. All I could get out of him was that he had got the girl drunk, and she had pulled a pistol and said he had killed her sister and she was going to kill him. He talked her out of shooting him, and meanwhile he gave her the whole five grains of morphine in a glass of whiskey. He said he went out to the kitchen for ice, with her following with the pistol, and made her a whiskey sour and stirred the morphine in without her ever catching on. Then she passed out—you know five grains will put anybody out in half an hour. He tore up the letter and sent it down the sewer. Then he laid her out on her bed, and finally got this idea of shooting her through the mouth to make it look like suicide. It was as far-fetched as his notion of burning up the house to cremate his wife and old Fox. The man was a killer at heart, that's all—and the mania cropped out. You know he killed a negro with a bale hook at the cotton gin near Palestine when he was just a kid?"

"I didn't know that," Lomax replied.

Potts' hatred of the more brilliant man he had lived on couldn't be downed. He went on.

"Oh, he was under sixteen and they claimed self-defense and got him off. But under all this society man and ornament to the bench and bar, there was a regular gorilla, I'll tell you."

The telephone rang. Lomax answered it.

"They want you, Hunt."

Andy talked in monosyllables for two minutes, ending with "I'll see you at the office. Potts has just spilled the works. Oh, just what we had figured out, principally. I'll tell you later; I've got to get over and write this for a new lead. Sure, I'm going extra again; it's good for another twenty thousand. All those bright reporters on the opposition rushed off after Morrison took the dive, and they haven't come back yet. So long."

Andy reached for his hat, on the far end of the table.

"Well, gentlemen, our friend Morrison has just died at St. Joseph's. Before he went out he managed to tell John Rorke, an interne and two nurses that he killed his wife, Martin Fox and Alice Blair. He seemed to be worried about Potts and O'Toole just before he died. A gentleman at the last, if not to the last. Coming, Sally?"

Sally was staring at Henry Potts. He had melted forward onto the table, his face buried between his limp hands.

"He's fainted," she gasped.

"Well, I'll have to get to the office," said Hunt. "See you there."

Sally saw her city editor much later. At the hospital, after they had put Potts to bed for his last sleep, John Rorke's always inquisitive fingers went through his pockets while the district attorney and his sister looked on. In a waistcoat pocket, were empty tubes that had held twenty grains of morphine. Mr. Potts, before confessing, had arranged his exit.

THE STUDIO
MURDER MYSTERY
THE EDINGTONS

THE COLUMNIST
MURDER

EXTRA!

LAWRENCE SAUNDERS

THE SEVEN BLACK
CHESSMEN
John Huntingdon

THE CASE OF THE
ADVERTISED
MURDER

MINNA BARDON

Coachwhip Publications
CoachwhipBooks.com

NOVEMBER JOE

DETECTIVE OF THE WOODS

H. HESKETH-PRICHARD

MURDER
IN A WALLED TOWN
KATHERINE WOODS

THE CAT SCREAMS
A HUGH RENNERT MYSTERY

TODD DOWNING

The Serpentine Club Investigates
Murder in Washington, D.C.

THE CAPITAL
MURDER

JAMES Z. ALNER

Coachwhip Publications
CoachwhipBooks.com

FEAR OF FEAR

FLORENCE RYERSON
COLIN CLEMENTS

MURDER IN THE FAMILY

NICE PEOPLE MURDER

Mary Hastings Bradley

3 DETECTIVES
FEMMES AUDACIEUSES
MERWIN · SOMERVILLE · FOOTNER

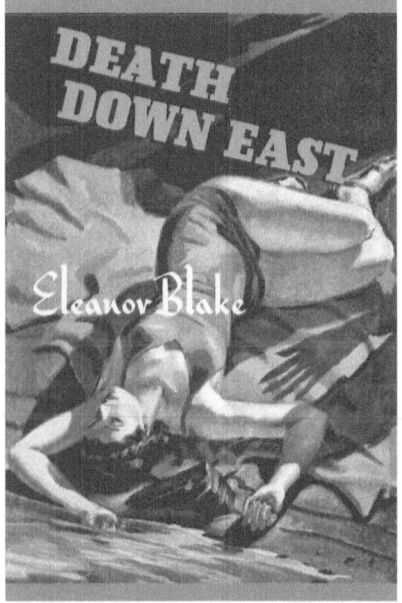

DEATH DOWN EAST

Eleanor Blake

Coachwhip Publications

CoachwhipBooks.com

THE
MYSTERY
OF THE
FOLDED
PAPER

HULBERT
FOOTNER

The
Hollow Tree
Mystery

MADELON ST. DENIS

VIRGINIA RATH

FERRYMAN,
TAKE HIM ACROSS!

No Face to
MURDER
EDITH HOWIE

Coachwhip Publications

CoachwhipBooks.com

THE QUINNY HITE
MYSTERIES
CHINESE RED · HERE LIES THE BODY

RICHARD BURKE

I'll Hate Myself in the Morning

Murder on the Left Bank

Elliot Paul

MURDER'S COMING

GRAVE WITHOUT GRASS

BY
DONALD CLOUGH CAMERON

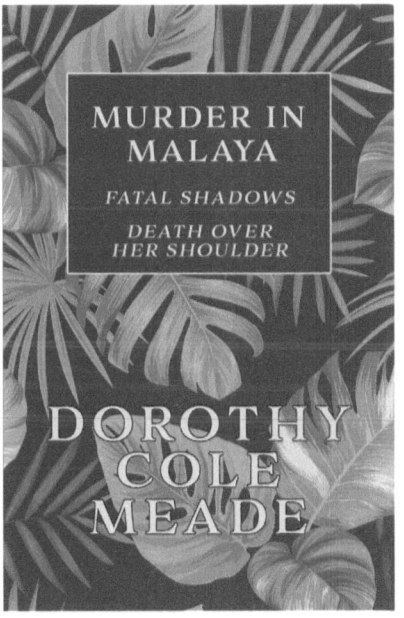

MURDER IN
MALAYA

FATAL SHADOWS

DEATH OVER
HER SHOULDER

DOROTHY
COLE
MEADE

Coachwhip Publications
CoachwhipBooks.com

MURDER
A LA
MODE

ELEANORE
KELLY
SELLARS

CLASSIC RED BADGE PRIZE MYSTERY

MURDER
ON THE
BLUFF

ESTHER TYLER

MURDER
BY JURY

MURDER
ON THE
APHRODITE

RUTH BURR SANBORN

LADIES
IN BOXES
GELETT
BURGESS

Coachwhip Publications

CoachwhipBooks.com

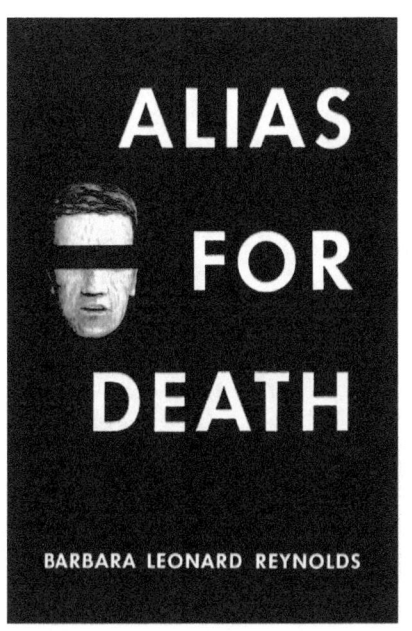

ALIAS FOR DEATH

BARBARA LEONARD REYNOLDS

THERE IS NO RETURN

THE ADELAIDE ADAMS MYSTERIES

ANITA BLACKMON

Jack Dolph

MURDER MAKES THE MARE GO

FEAR CAME FIRST

VERA KELSEY

Coachwhip Publications

CoachwhipBooks.com

MURDER AT DRAKE'S ANCHORAGE

E. LEE WADDELL

MURDER AT THE KENTUCKY DERBY

CHARLES PARMER

MURDER ENDS THE SONG

ALFRED MEYERS

3 DETECTIVES
MURDER ON THE RAILS
WHITECHURCH • THORNE • TORGERSON

Coachwhip Publications

CoachwhipBooks.com

THE FIRES AT
FITCH'S FOLLY

KENNETH WHIPPLE

DRESSED
TO KILL

Emma Lou Fetta

GRIM
DEATH

THE
GROUSE
MOOR
MURDER

JOHN FERGUSON

Coachwhip Publications

CoachwhipBooks.com

www.ingramcontent.com/pod-product-compliance
Lightning Source LLC
Chambersburg PA
CBHW020610250626
47154CB00004B/1447